"Alone at last," Richard said

He transferred his smile and his full attention to Joanna.

"You call this alone?" she asked dryly, looking around the tables. Other diners at the hotel seemed to be lingering overlong with their coffee, casting surreptitious glances at the famous man in their midst.

"It happens in this business." Richard's mouth took a bittersweet tilt. "I suppose I've learned to just block the attention out."

"Fiddlesticks!" Joanna was unimpressed by the pathos adopted for her benefit. "You thrive on an audience."

"Fiddlesticks?" he murmured, delighted by the old-fashioned term. Then he admitted, unabashed, "Most of the time I don't mind an audience, but there are times when I revere privacy." His eyes locked with hers, his voice becoming seductively quiet. "Why were you at the premiere that night?"

SUSAN NAPIER was born on Valentine's Day, so perhaps it is only fitting that she should become a romance writer. She started out as a reporter for New Zealand's largest evening newspaper before resigning to marry the paper's chief reporter. After the birth of their two children she did some freelancing for a film production company and then settled down to write her first romance. "Now," she says, "I am in the enviable position of being able to build my career around my home and family."

Books by Susan Napier

HARLEQUIN PRESENTS
885—SWEET AS MY REVENGE
924—THE COUNTERFEIT SECRETARY
940—THE LONELY SEASON

HARLEQUIN ROMANCE
2711—LOVE IN THE VALLEY
2723—SWEET VIXEN

Don't miss any of our special offers. Write to us at the following address for information on our newest releases.

Harlequin Reader Service
901 Fuhrmann Blvd., P.O. Box 1397, Buffalo, NY 14240
Canadian address: P.O. Box 603,
Fort Erie, Ont. L2A 5X3

SUSAN NAPIER

true enchanter

Harlequin Books

TORONTO • NEW YORK • LONDON
AMSTERDAM • PARIS • SYDNEY • HAMBURG
STOCKHOLM • ATHENS • TOKYO • MILAN

He is the true enchanter, whose spell
operates, not upon the senses, but
upon the imagination and the heart.
                                    Washington Irving

Harlequin Presents first edition February 1988
ISBN 0-373-11051-0

Original hardcover edition published in 1987
by Mills & Boon Limited

CHAPTER ONE

'Miss Carson! Miss Carson!' The small, dark-haired girl with one furtively pierced ear tried to attract the attention of the nervous figure in the goal-mouth.

'Not now, Teresa!' cried Joanna out of the corner of her mouth, keeping her attention firmly fixed on the field. 'I've got to concentrate. We're losing by miles, and if I let any more goals through I'm going to be sidelined in disgrace.'

The sad fact was that she would probably be sidelined anyway. She usually was. Her life-long enthusiasm for sport had never been matched by her abilities, and her short-sightedness and suspect depth-perception had always made her a reluctant last choice when it came to picking teams for games. As a child she had compensated by competing at everything with almost suicidal fervour, but at twenty-three she was resigned to playing badly, no matter how determined her efforts. Still, her enthusiasm never flagged and she suspected it was for that alone that she had been seconded to the teachers' team for the end-of-term teachers versus pupils hockey match. It had been thought—wrongly, as it was turning out—that tucked away in the goal she could do relatively little damage.

'But, Miss Carson, Mr McKinlay sent me to get you,' Teresa wailed.

'I can't come now,' Joanna panted, running back and forth in front of the net in eager frustration as a great mauling pack of bodies bristling with waving sticks came barrelling down the playing-field towards her.

'But you *have* to!' Teresa, whose laziness in class was legendary, actually managed to sound urgent. 'There's someone here to see you.'

'Well, they'll have to wait.' Joanna frantically hitched up

7

the pads which tended to keep sliding down her too-slender legs and tripping her up.

'He can't. He's in a terrible hurry—has to catch a plane or something. You have to come. *Please*, Miss Carson.'

'Who is it, do you know?' Joanna squinted through the wire-rimmed granny glasses selected to match the traditional staff-team ensemble of black gym-slip and stockings, wishing she had kept her lenses in. A battered panama hat sank low over her ears, a further handicap with its sloppily dipping brim. The approaching mêlée was getting dangerously close. This was her big chance to make a dramatic save—but where was the ball? Oh, no! She blinked with horror. The captain of the First Eleven had it!

'It's Richard Marlow, the film star!' shrieked Teresa in her high treble, unable to keep her excitement to herself any longer. Joanna's head snapped sideways.

'*What?*'

Disaster struck with unspeakable speed. A loud thwack sounded in her ear, and as her head swung back the ball whistled past her cheek with such force that it flipped out of the net and caught Joanna sharply on the back of the neck. She yelped, and tears came to her eyes to blur the sudden vision of stars. She tripped over her trailing pad and laid herself out on the battered grass, hardly hearing the chorus of cheers from the watching students and the groans of her team-mates.

'Oh, gosh! Sorry, Miss Carson,' the captain said cheerfully. 'I thought you were going to jump out of the way, like last time.'

'Last time the ball was incoming, not outgoing.' Joanna sat up to rub her neck, still dazed by the speed of the calamity. 'I didn't expect it to sneak up behind me.'

'That was quite a thump you got,' said the Home Economics teacher sympathetically. 'You'd better knock off for a while ... let someone else take a turn in goal.'

Looking at her colleagues' relieved grins, Joanna picked herself haughtily off the grass. 'If that was my ball, I'd take it home with me,' she said huffily, as she struggled with the buckles of her pads.

'No, you wouldn't, you're too good a sport,' chuckled the teacher who was taking over her position. 'You're a very graceful loser.'

'I get lots of practise,' said Joanna feelingly, as she departed the scene of her ignominy, the stiffening tissues of her neck hampering her attempts at dignity.

'Miss Carson——' Teresa's anxious whine reminded her of the unwelcome cause of her downfall.

Richard Marlow. Wretched man! For someone whom she hadn't even met yet, he was causing her an awful lot of trouble. At first it had seemed like a terrific opportunity— to tutor/chaperon her seventeen-year-old niece on a movie location for several weeks. Rebecca had been chosen from among hundreds of schoolgirl hopefuls to take the female lead in *The Woodturner*, the latest film directed by Richard Marlow, but her mother had only let her audition on the understanding that she would not neglect her schoolwork, and continue with her plans for University.

Thinking of her sister made Joanna sigh. Ellen was a chronic worrier, beautiful but highly-strung, and definitely over-protective as a mother. The accidental conception of Sam, delivered four months ago just before her fortieth birthday, had made her even worse. Initially, she had been pleased by her daughter's success, but lately she had been harbouring dark thoughts about the advisability of letting her darling daughter loose among amoral actors and film people. To make matters worse, Becky had become infatuated with Richard Marlow, and the relationship between mother and daughter, already strained by the similarity in their characters, was stretched to breaking-point. Ellen claimed that Richard Marlow was encouraging the infatuation with reckless disregard for her daughter's innocence, and Becky claimed that her mother was merely jealous. Joanna fought hard to remain strictly neutral, but she was losing patience with both of them.

'. . . Miss Carson?'

'What? Oh, yes, Teresa?' Joanna realised she was being addressed. She tucked the hockey stick under her arm, and tried to smooth out the baggy knees of her stockings as she half jogged, half walked between the blocks of classrooms with her excited pupil.

'I just wondered . . .' Teresa was being suspiciously diffident '. . . I mean, I didn't like to ask with Mr McKinlay there, and him being in such a rush and all, and I'm supposed to go straight back to Art class . . . Do you think . . .? Do you suppose . . . since you'll be working for him . . .' She took a breath and wound up to the big burst: 'Could you get his autograph for me?' Teresa thrust a pad and pencil at Joanna and darted quickly away, tossing back a breathless, 'Thanks *awfully*, Miss Carson!'

If only she was always so eager to get to class, thought Joanna wryly, wishing her pupils weren't all such avid movie fans. Ever since they had learned about her connection with *The Woodturner* they had driven her mad with questions and pleas for autographs. She certainly wasn't going to have trouble signing people up for the video classes she was planning on her return. She trotted on, slowing as she realised what kind of first impression she was going to make. Perhaps she should at least take off the awful panama.

As she rounded the corner of the assembly hall she saw a tall, red-headed figure limping across the quadrangle towards a yellow car idling in the staff car-park. She recognised him instantly, remembering the times she had seen him move fluidly across stage and screen, before the car accident that had ended his headlong assault on international stardom, and seen the beginning of his directing career.

'Mr Marlow? Mr Marlow!' She put on a spurt as she called.

He broke stride to look behind him. At the sight of the skinny schoolgirl, all knees and elbows, racing towards him, he picked up his pace.

'Mr Marlow!' Joanna's voice rang shrill with puffed annoyance, but he kept going, hardly using the stick in his left hand. For a man who was supposed to be crippled he had a pretty turn of speed! She caught up with him just as he made the car-park pavement: 'Mr Marlow——'

'Not now, honey,' he smiled dazzlingly into thin air, 'I'm in a hurry.'

'I know,' she panted, not willing to give up when she'd got this far. She'd expected someone from the film company to contact her about the job that Ellen had insisted she take, but she hadn't expected it to be the Great Man himself. Becky was always on about how *frantically* busy he was, how *horrendously* pressured. Joanna didn't know how good an actress her niece was, but she could certainly dramatise . . . almost as well as her mother!

'Mr Marlow——' She tried again, half turning and trotting backwards to keep up with his slowed stride, and the hockey stick dangling forgotten from her hand bumped against her leg, rebounded off his walking-stick and caught him a crack across the shins. He stumbled, and with a startled curse almost sprawled at her feet.

'Oh, God,' she moaned, trying to help him regain his balance. 'I'm so sorry, I only wanted to ask you——'

'Oh, give me the damned thing!' His eyes glittered like broken green glass as he snatched the pad and pencil out of her hand. 'What's your name?'

'Jo—er . . . make it to Teresa,' Joanna stammered, taken aback by the suddenness of his action. She stared, speechless, as he quickly scrawled across the paper. The hand that held the pencil had an almost feminine grace and slenderness, but there was nothing feminine about the whipcord body, or the hard muscles revealed by the tight jeans as he bent a knee to provide support for the pad. She couldn't help noticing that his lashes and brows were as thick as the shockingly red hair, but darker in hue, and the skin stretched over the long, narrow jaw was smooth and supple, unmarred by a single freckle. He was wearing a warm, spicy cologne, a faintly familiar fragrance that made Joanna want to lean closer to inhale it. She felt the tiny tug at her senses with dismay, and then the pad was back in her hand and she was watching him retreat.

'Mr Marlow, please wait, I'm——'

He cut her off with a quick, blinding smile that side-slipped off his preoccupied face. 'Look, darling, if it's about my film, I finished casting ages ago. And if it's about an acting career I can't help you. There aren't any short cuts, not if you want to be good. It's all work, and hard work at that, and it never stops . . . which is why I must run . . .'

'Mr Marlow——' She could have screamed with frustration. He wasn't listening to her any more than he was really looking at her. Knowing actors, those green eyes probably only saw reflections of himself anyway! She was about to howl out that she was his new star's aunt, when suddenly he stooped and closed off her breath with a kiss . . . a swift, meaningless salute of the lips followed by another brilliant, blind smile. 'Something else to tell your friends.'

Joanna gaped at him as he escaped the last ten metres to the waiting car, which screeched away from the kerb before he'd even closed the door.

Egomaniac! Joanna's mouth snapped shut. OK, in the circumstances it was fair enough that he should mistake her for a schoolgirl, but did it naturally follow that every schoolgirl was panting for a display of cheap, matinée-idol charm? If he had bothered to look at her properly instead of trying to fend her off with false smiles, he would have seen that she was a mature woman, not an over-heated teenager on the rampage!

'Did you see what that brat did to me?' Richard Marlow rubbed his aching shins, and glared at the grinning man clashing the gears.

'I thought it was a very novel way of capturing your fleeing attention.' Dean Jacobs tried to straighten his mouth. 'Involving as it did her remaining completely clothed!'

Richard gave the big, blond American a weary look. 'Is that story still doing the rounds?'

'Which one? There are so many,' Dean gibed. 'Did you see the aunt?'

'No, I did not see the aunt,' said Richard tiredly. 'But I did see dozens of budding Sarah Bernhardts, gathering and hovering with giggling menace. It was a scene straight out of *The Birds*, so, being a Hitchcock fan, I took the hint and ran. I nearly made it, too, until that skinny black crow descended and nearly pecked me to death.'

Dean gave a rolling laugh. 'I didn't think schoolgirls dressed like that any more . . . jolly hockey sticks and all. So what do you want to do now?'

Richard shrugged. 'Catch my plane. It's not as if we've got a choice about having the aunt as chaperon. Whether I like her or not, Ellen Turner is insisting—Lord save me from stage mothers! How unsuitable can she be, anyway? Ellen says she's a dedicated teacher, used to getting respect from her pupils. A nice, sensible maiden aunt with a schoolmarm air is probably the best thing for Becky—and she has the added advantage of knowing exactly who she's taking on. I only hope that her sister hasn't primed her to interfere. While I'm away you or Toni can set her straight on that. Have a nice chat over the teacups and let her know that, family or not, she's being paid to look after Becky's physical and scholastic welfare, not to have any artistic opinions.'

'And I suppose that if she does develop any obstructive scruples you'll be forced to use some of that meagre store of charm of yours,' said Dean slyly, 'to cajole her into a state of undying loyalty? Perhaps even a tiny part as an extra somewhere . . .?'

'You, my friend, are going to make an excellent director one day,' Richard murmured, with his first gleam of real humour. 'Meantime, remember that for the moment you're only my assistant. *I* come up with the brilliantly devious schemes, and *you* carry them out.'

'Does that mean what I think it means?' asked Dean suspiciously.

Richard's mobile mouth began a slow slide at his reaction. 'It means, dear boy, that if the schoolmarm starts to make waves, you may have to temporarily forget the lovely Loren in make-up, and devote your *meagre* cowboy charm to keeping her happy and off your boss's back.'

He began to laugh. There were long months of intensive work ahead of them, during which he knew he would badly need the perspective of his humour. He was psyched up for the physical and emotional turbulence that always accompanied a sustained creative effort, even looking forward to the challenging problems that would arise. But, ultimately, nothing would be allowed to stand in the way of his film.

'I guess I'll just have to hope she's as gorgeous-looking as her sister,' Dean said wryly. 'Though with my luck she'll turn out to be the elder, and all those statuesque family proportions will have run to middle-age spread!'

Joanna—to whom puberty had been an anticlimax, as all her friends blossomed into womanly curves while she remained boyishly flat—found amusement finally conquering her pique. Her class would be up in arms to discover how brutally she had treated their favourite TV and movie star. She shuddered to think what would happen if she confessed that tripping him up had gained her an autograph *and* an unsolicited kiss. They'd be out there on the streets in a flash, looking for celebrities to beat up!

She looked at the autograph, her grin fading. *To Teresa, with all my love, Richard Marlow. All* my love? She sniffed. Could he possibly have any left, the way the papers had him throwing it around so indiscriminately? How predictable was that scribble, and how crass . . . and how Teresa would swoon!

In spite of herself, she was beginning to look forward to

her formal introduction to the utterly wonderful Mr Marlow. She would have the element of surprise on her side, if nothing else. It would be rather pleasant to disconcert a man who seemed to take it for granted that every woman he met was ready and willing to lie down and let him walk all over her.

She recalled their first, and only, fleeting encounter before this one. It had been the previous week at a charity film première which she had attended with Duncan McKinlay. As well as being the headmaster of one of the largest state secondary schools in Auckland, Duncan was involved with numerous charities, and as their professional relationship strengthened and became more personal, Joanna had accompanied him to quite a few social functions.

She had been dressed, and waiting for Duncan to arrive at her flat, when Ellen rang to tell her that Becky would be at the première too—with Richard Marlow.

'He said it was publicity—to show her off—but you know what Becky's like, she's taking it all personally.' Ellen's voice held the aggrieved note it always acquired these days when she referred to her daughter. 'She thinks it's all so glamorous and exciting. Well, maybe it is at the moment, but what's going to happen afterwards, that's what I want to know? What happens when filming's over and she has to go back to being an ordinary schoolgirl again? I tell her she's just storing up grief for herself but, of course, she doesn't hear me. Richard can do no wrong as far as she's concerned. She'd jump over a cliff if he told her to.'

Joanna bit her tongue to stop herself telling Ellen she should have thought all this over before she and her husband signed the film company contract on Becky's behalf. If truth be told, they had probably been a little dazzled by the glamour of it all, too, but any suggestion of it would start a row. Ellen was as sensitive to criticism these days as she was to references about her age, or hints that Becky might respond better to a lightening of the maternal hand on the leading strings.

In spite of her determination not to let Ellen's attitude
cloud her judgement, Joanna found herself rather
anxiously searching the crowd after the première. He
wasn't difficult to find . . . even in the midst of a flamboyant
and entertaining gathering, Richard Marlow managed to
stand out as a centre of interest.

He was tall, but it wasn't his height that drew and held
people's attention, it was a kind of presence, an aura of
arrogant carelessness that was simultaneously both unselfconscious and studied. Seeing him in the flesh, even across
the room, gave Joanna an odd warning prickle. He looked
leaner and harder than he had seemed in his last film. His
skin was startlingly pale under the unflattering overhead
lights, his hair a violent flame. He was propped up against a
fluted column in the foyer, champagne in one hand, the
ever-present stick in the other, totally at ease holding court
in the limelight, drinking in the attention of an admiring
half-circle of men and women with every indication of
enjoyment. A born performer, Joanna decided, having
known a few in her time. They were always playing to an
audience, even if it was only an audience of one.
Everything was grist to an actor's mill, and woe betide the
girl who mistook their dramatics for genuine emotion.

That Rebecca was in the grip of genuine emotion was
distressingly in evidence. There was sheer hero-worship in
her wide, blue eyes as she gazed adoringly at her mentor.
Her dress was a shade too old for her, thought Joanna
critically, although the shimmering hot pink went perfectly with the long, honey-blonde hair. She clung to
Richard Marlow's elbow with a mixture of pride,
excitement and anxiety mingling on her lovely young face.
Joanna felt a pang of guilt at having dismissed Ellen's fears
so summarily to date. Perhaps they weren't all self-
generated.

'Why don't you go over and say hello?' Duncan's
murmur disturbed her niggling thoughts.

'No, thanks.' Joanna dragged her eyes off the couple

across the room and looked at Duncan. A former rugby player, he was square and sturdy, with a rugged face that bordered on the ugly. But he was a straightforward and honest man, gentle and kind and with a heart of pure gold. Joanna was almost certain that she was in love with him. Certainly, she enjoyed his company, and he made her feel warm, secure and happy.

'Why not?' Duncan asked her fondly. 'You *are* Becky's aunt, and she does look a little out of her depth in that sophisticated crowd. Mind you, you can't really claim that Marlow's not looking after her.'

Perhaps too well, thought Joanna, her brow creasing as she looked over again to see the man in question listening in an attitude of indulgent respect to a bubbling Becky. A man of his experience couldn't help but be aware of Becky's feelings, they were naked in her face. But was he really exploiting Becky's emotional vulnerability for the sake of his film, as Ellen claimed, with a total disregard for the consequences?

'You *are* going to chaperon her, aren't you, Joanna?' Duncan had noted her wavering expression. 'Don't let Ellen put you off. It really is a marvellous opportunity for you, considering that you're our resident drama expert. And with the holidays coming up you won't be missing more than a couple of weeks of school. You might even be able to persuade one or two of the production crew to come and give us some lectures about film careers.'

'If only Ellen wasn't complicating matters with this bee in her bonnet——'

'Ellen always has a bee in her bonnet about something; it's not infectious, you know. Do what you want to do. And you don't even have to worry about your kids. When the holiday's over I'll put them straight into their work skills programme . . . providing, of course, that you've done your job well enough that they're *capable* of holding down a job for two consecutive weeks!'

Joanna bristled for a moment on behalf of her much-maligned 'special' class of fifth-formers, before she realised that she was being gently teased. 'Ellen will kill me if I go and Becky gets up to any mischief.'

'She'll kill you anyway if you *don't* go,' Duncan pointed out with a grin, knowing how Joanna hated being put under pressure by her sister, but also knowing that she really wanted to watch a film company in action. 'Now, are you absolutely certain that you don't want to go over and introduce yourself?'

'I don't think I should interrupt the performance,' said Joanna drily. She shrank from the idea of invading the limelight. 'Besides ... I have this thing about red hair. When I was four the little red-headed boy next door persuaded me to let him scalp me—and *I* was the one to get the spanking. I've never trusted anyone with red hair since.'

Duncan returned her grin. 'He didn't come back for a re-match in the last fortnight by any chance?'

'Not unless he's had a sex change and dyed his hair.' Joanna ruffled the haircut that had caused such a fuss among her friends. Her hair wasn't the honey-blonde of her sister and niece, but a smoky silver and so fine as to be almost unmanageable. She had always worn it tied back, but on her last visit to the hairdresser she had made the mistake of telling the trendy young stylist to 'do something different', and compounded it by taking out her lenses, since any kind of chemical or cosmetic irritated them. When she had replaced them later she had nearly died. Her hair had been razor-cut to an inch all over, emphasising the bones and angles of her narrow face with uncompromising starkness. Ellen had hated it, which had instantly made Joanna defensive. Now she liked it ... the androgynous look was perfect for her figure ... or lack of it.

Duncan chuckled. It had taken him a while to get used to her hair but, as long as she was happy with it, so was he. Right now, in her long, clinging white dress, she looked deceptively fragile and, even though she had moaned about having to wear spectacles because of her make-up, he thought that she looked quite pretty, in an unusual kind of way.

'How about we circulate a bit and spread the word about the next fund-raising effort?' he suggested. 'And if you do happen to get close enough to Becky ... well ...'

With the possibility firmly in the back of her mind, Joanna duly circulated and began to enjoy herself as she met up with several people she hadn't seen since her days with the University theatre group.

One vaguely familiar face turned out to be Nick Fellows, whom she had dated a few times. He was still husky and good-looking, and volunteered the information that he had a small part in *The Woodturner*.

'Only five days' work, and New Plymouth this time of year can be damned bitter, but it's work none the less and it'll make a change from my hack-work in the TV soaps.'

It was the perfect opportunity. Nick had always been a terrible gossip, and when Joanna mentioned her own probable behind-the-scenes involvement he was extremely forthcoming.

'I worked with Richard Marlow lots of times when he was still doing theatre—a great guy, loaded with temperament but I suppose you couldn't expect much else with his background. What have the Marlows got ... two actresses, two directors, an artist and a rock singer in the family?'

'Something like that,' Joanna murmured dutifully. Actress Constance Marlow and her actor/writer/director husband, Michael, still led very active careers and appeared almost as often in the news as their colourful offspring. 'Has he changed much, do you think?'

'Since those days? Quite a bit. He used to be quite fun, but hellishly undisciplined ... sparks shooting out all over the place. More mature now, I suppose, and I guess that accident slowed him up a bit, physically anyway ... except where women are concerned ...' He gave Joanna a sly wink. 'Always liked variety, did Richard.'

'He did get engaged,' Joanna felt constrained to point out.

'Got unengaged too, fairly rapidly, poor sod—that's one subject that he's not very expansive on.'

Joanna couldn't blame him. It must have dented his ego, if not his heart, to have his fiancée, co-star Bianca James, run off and marry his best friend while Richard was still anchored by a chest-to-toe cast to an LA hospital bed. It must have been salt in the wound when Finn Tracey got not only Bianca, but also the role Richard had contracted to play in a new film . . . a macho action-adventure which had turned out to be a box-office smash.

'He can't be too bitter about it if he's willing to cast Finn Tracey as the lead in *The Woodturner*,' she said.

'Don't think he had much choice. He wanted to use all unknowns in the cast but the backers insisted on a big name, and you don't get much bigger than Finn. Also, he can act. Even if Richard personally hates his guts, he'll bury it for the sake of his film and maybe, since Bianca is off filming somewhere in Europe, there won't be any open points of conflict. Hope not, because Richard needs this one to establish his reputation. I mean, I know that first film he directed was a critical and commercial success, but in this business that's no guarantee. Some people would delight in seeing him fall flat on his face.'

They had drifted as they talked, and when Nick espied another long-lost friend, Joanna turned to find herself on the very edge of the group which currently surrounded Richard Marlow. She felt a tiny shock of surprise and then was annoyed with herself. Why should *she* feel nervous?

The green eyes which had flashed so brilliantly at a distance and appeared so soulful on screen looked even more jewel-like at close quarters. He was holding forth again and it was another shock to hear that smooth, slick voice in ordinary conversation. He wasn't thirty yet, but his voice seemed to encompass a world of ageless mystery and poetical experience. So distracted was she by the musical voice that Joanna missed the interruption by the voluptuous brunette who had insinuated herself in front of him.

Whatever the interruption was, it was unwelcome, for Joanna saw Richard Marlow's face stiffen slightly. He shook his head and murmured something in a low voice, but the woman persisted, leaning towards him, swaying suggestively against him. He didn't move, but Joanna saw a flicker of distaste touch the deep green eyes, and his lean, well-defined shoulders shrugged with apparent carelessness. He said something briefly and the woman jerked back a step. Then she, too, shrugged.

There was a gasp as the bodice of the woman's slinky, ice-blue dress slid beautifully down the slope of her upper arms with an ease that Joanna suspected was rehearsed. If her front was as perfectly shaped as the creamy curve of her back then Richard Marlow must really be getting an eyeful, thought Joanna numbly, unable to believe that this was actually happening in public. Luckily, they were off centre-stage but there were still enough people in the corner alcove to create a scandalised ripple.

An expectant hush settled over the half-embarrassed, half-avid audience. Green eyes glittered in an expressionless mask, then they dipped, and rose again to the lady's face.

'Very impressive, my dear,' he drawled, on such an exquisite note of boredom that Joanna felt a chill down her spine, '. . . but can they *act*?'

A graceful turn and he had scooped up a wildly blushing Rebecca and limped through the parting crowd to the bar, leaving the half-naked woman surrounded by snickers of uneasy laughter. A man, her escort, judging by his angry flush, hustled her away, ignoring her shrill protests.

Joanna was furious. How dared he expose Rebecca to such a cruel display! The foolish woman had asked for everything she got, but there had been other ways for Richard Marlow to defuse the moment. Why hadn't he just turned away without saying anything? Or dismissed the moment lightly instead of making it a public execution? Did he enjoy humiliating women? Or had he simply not been able to resist playing to the expectant gallery? And this was the man who was playing Svengali to Rebecca's innocent Trilby! She frowned blackly at the back of the flame-red head where it had paused by the bar . . . was he pouring more champagne into Becky? Unexpectedly, he turned, and with a jolt she found herself glaring into fathomless eyes.

One red brow flicked up as his eyes roved past, to the place where the little drama had been staged. When he looked back at her, instead of shame or ruefulness, his eyes were filled with a kind of amused challenge, as if he was daring her to disapprove of his behaviour, confident that she would not. In parody of his action of a few moments ago, he looked down at her breasts.

At the sight of the two small bumps barely visible under the smooth line of her tube dress, a grin of pure enchantment overtook the slightly bored amusement quirking his mouth. His eyes meshed with hers again, the green alight with such a pied piper's lilt of delighted laughter that for an instant Joanna was unbearably tempted to follow it with laughter of her own. So tempted that she was shocked at succumbing so easily to his charm when he was actually *mocking* her. He was comparing her to that busty brunette! To her outrage, he winked sympathetically.

Her face hot, she turned and presented him with offended shoulder-blades jutting out like little flightless wings against the rigid line of her back bone. She might be thin, and her wearing of a bra merely a courtesy gesture towards underwear manufacturers but, after all, thinness was fashionable! How dare he make her feel that she was sadly lacking! Simmering, she set off to find Duncan, trying to shake off the awful feeling that every eye in the place was fixed critically on the smallness of her breasts.

She would have been further fortified if she'd known what thoughts had drifted through Richard Marlow's mind as he watched her stalk away. He had been thoroughly out of humour. Nadia had been drunk of course, but that didn't excuse her stupid stunt. He had known it would take something short and sharp to penetrate that alcoholic haze—God knows what she might have done if he'd attempted to be pleasant. That she was beautiful didn't alter the fact that the only talent she had was for exhibitionism, and he wasn't about to be manipulated so easily.

It had taken the outraged owl to restore his humour. She had bristled so fiercely, as if Nadia were an innocent chick in need of protection instead of a woman whose reputation was notorious even in a profession renowned for its liberal morality. A snowy owl, with that incredibly cropped silver hair and the big hazel eyes magnified behind the oval frames, and he had ruffled her feathers by smiling at her little breasts. That she hadn't been a model, or an actress, was evident by her offended response . . . but what a Peter Pan she would make! he thought, as she turned that fragile body away, giving him a brief glimpse of a delicate profile, or an Ariel . . . a sexless imp as light and gauzy as a morning mist. Yet such delicacy rarely succeeded in projecting itself on stage or screen and, anyway, snowy owls were rare and belonged safe in the wild, not frozen in the relentless glare of a spotlight.

Lovely are the curves of the white owl sweeping
Wavy in the dusk lit by one large star.

The lines by Meredith wandered unbidden out of his memory, and the irony of it made him smile. This owl *had* no curves to speak of and, as for stars—his mouth tightened cynically—his own might be on the wane if he didn't pull this picture off. A director was only as good as his last film.

Joanna didn't mention to Ellen her brief brush with Richard Marlow, but she did finally make the firm commitment to take on the chaperoning job, impelled by a sense of righteous indignation.

Now, as she made her way to Duncan's office, she was determined to make sure that Becky's youthful ego didn't suffer too badly at the hands of Richard Marlow's super-inflated one!

'Oh, Lord, Joanna!' Duncan looked appalled when he saw her St Trinian's garb. 'I forgot about the game. Maybe its lucky you missed Marlow after all.'

'What did he want?' asked Joanna, not wanting to correct him and turn herself into fodder for staff-room amusement for the next few weeks.

'Just an introduction, and to leave these schedules and information sheets for you.' He handed her a thick file from his desk. 'He said that he really would have liked to see you, Ellen and Becky together, but that the weather had been causing some changes in his schedule. He's on his way to New Plymouth now and wasn't sure when he'd be back again; only dropped in because we're on the way to the airport. He said someone from the production office would be in touch with you. And he asked what you were like as a teacher.'

'What did you say?'

Duncan grinned happily. 'The truth—that you're a valuable member of staff, that I trust your teaching instincts implicitly . . . that your techniques seemed to get through to even the most hardened of our young delinquents. That you're practical, realistic and down-to-earth.'

'Can I have that in writing?'

'Any time. Actually, he wasn't at all what I expected, very natural and unaffected . . . rather likeable in fact.' Duncan sounded surprised at himself and Joanna hid a grin. His opinion of actors as people was not very high—he suspected them as either being effeminate or degenerate.

'I'm sure he meant to be,' she murmured, tempted to ask if Duncan had got a kiss too, but controlling the wicked impulse.

'Mmmm. I was going to mention about the lectures, see if he could recommend someone or even come himself, but unfortunately 3D girls arrived to learn about the Gestetner, and I think he found them a bit unnerving.'

No wonder he had moved so fast, Joanna thought in amusement. The hungry little souls of 3D girls were enough to unnerve anybody, even a man who had made a living out of satisfying hungry female fantasies.

'Never mind, it's probably better to wait,' Duncan continued. 'You can get to know a few of the people involved, find out what sort of thing will fit into the syllabus. And maybe Marlow would be more co-operative for someone who's not asking him cold.'

Maybe ... and maybe not. Joanna had the distinct feeling that she and Richard Marlow were not destined to be fast friends. At the end of nine weeks they would probably be glad to see the back of each other!

CHAPTER TWO

'Am I going to get some quiet back there? Or shall we all just pack up and go home and collect the unemployment benefit?'

Hands on slim hips, Richard Marlow watched the result of his sweetly caustic snarl on the chattering group of people gathered around the small semicircle of utility vans. When the silence was complete he surveyed them expressively for a few moments.

'Thank you.' The sarcasm was weighted silk. 'I realise that for many of you all this is very ho-hum, but you're *supposed* to be professionals. For those of you who seem to have forgotten, that——' an outflung hand, '——is a microphone. It picks up sound—any sound. When I call for quiet on-set I am *not* joking.' He paused, eyebrows raised for objections. When there were none he continued, 'Now, if you can bear to control your stifling boredom for a little longer I *might* be able to prevail upon Mr Tracey to remember his lines long enough for us to get a take.'

A dig and slash of the stick at his side pivoted him back to the action, his other hand pinching the bridge of his nose in an attitude of long-suffering disgust. If Joanna hadn't been admiring the effectiveness of his sarcastic performance she might have sympathised with him. In the two hours that she and Becky had been on location very little seemed to have been achieved, and the tension was mounting appreciably.

'Uh—oh.' Someone behind Joanna dared break the silence with a whisper. 'We're cooking, guys.'

'Five bucks on Dean,' a female voice muttered, and was followed by a breathy flurry of other, cryptic bets, as the camera began to roll again at a sharp command.

Joanna watched as Finn Tracey, seated on the sagging veranda steps of a tumbledown wooden shack, launched into the long monologue that was causing the problem. His coal-black hair and beard were long and matted, his clothes unkempt, and the scars that puckered the skin on one side of his face and one arm were stomach-turning masterpieces of make-up design.

Finn was playing the part of David, a sculptor who has been physically and emotionally scarred in a fire which has killed his wife and child. Haunted by nightmares, he has turned his back on his life and art by retreating to a remote rural community, where he scrapes a bare living for himself by carving wooden furniture. But even there he is the object of curiosity, and the hostility of a tightly knit community which is suspicious of anyone who is 'different'.

Rebecca's character, Helen, was that of a girl on the

brink of womanhood, trapped there by an over-protective brother and her own unquestioning acceptance of a rigid, isolated upbringing.

At their first, accidental, encounter, Helen is repelled by David's appearance, but she comes to be fascinated by the bitter man behind the ugly mask. Her innocent pity turns to something else as she struggles with the conflicts of fear and curiosity ... at this point the film became a study of the slow and painful development of a relationship between a man who believes that life is over and a young woman for whom it is just beginning. Through the innocently passionate love which Helen offers, David rediscovers his capacity for feeling, and thus his creative spirit. But darker emotions are at work in Helen's brother, Michael. He has his own obsessions about the relationship, which erupt violently one night and result in a tense, terrifying hunt through the bush. Michael is killed but although the lovers survive there is no conventional happy ending. They part at a station—Helen to spread her wings in a world that David has made her realise exists outside the false security of the familiar—and David to return to the art he had abandoned ... It was left up to the audience to decide whether they would ever meet again. Joanna, for her part, had firmly decided that they would. The script was intelligent and sensitive, allowing each character growth and complexity and, looking across at Becky's rapt face, Joanna hoped that she would be able to live up to the material. Becky herself seemed to have no doubts, looking forward to her role with eager excitement. When they had boarded the plane at Auckland airport that morning for the fifty-minute flight to New Plymouth, Rebecca had been bubbling over with relief at being on her way at last.

'Thank goodness you're coming with me and not Mum,' she had burst out as they had taxied away from the last view of the distant, tearful figure of anxious motherhood. 'She's such a nag! I was terrified that she'd change her mind at the last minute, and find someone to baby-sit Sam while she came along. It would have been so *humiliating*, turning up on location with my *mother* in tow . . .'

'Brooke Shields does it,' Joanna pointed out drily. 'Besides, is an aunt much better?'

'Oh, *yes*. Anyway, you don't *act* like an aunt, if you know what I mean. You don't look like anybody's aunt either—or even a school teacher for that matter.' She giggled as Joanna straightened her shoulders in an attempt to look taller than her niece, who topped her by a couple of centimetres. 'Remember when you met Dean? He said that Mum hadn't told them you were her *baby* sister. I think he was expecting someone more like her.'

'Then he was definitely disappointed, wasn't he?' murmured Joanna, who hadn't ever been really jealous of her sister's looks. For one thing, Ellen had to watch her diet, which would have been a constitutional impossibility for Joanna, who was *always* hungry. For another, Joanna's tomboyish looks and personality complemented each other perfectly . . . she always had too many things to do to waste time primping in the mirror, or worrying about her face or hair or nails. As for clothes . . . she had long given up trying to look sexy. She could wear a dress slashed to the navel and look about as sexy as a clothes-peg!

Wriggling in the canvas chair that had jokingly been produced by Dean with the legend 'Teach' printed across the back support, Joanna missed the initial explosion.

When she looked up Richard Marlow was towering over the small, untidy young woman who had aborted yet another take with an ill-timed cough. It was his production assistant, Toni Fields, and Joanna almost blanched at the avalanche of eloquent insults that were being heaped on her bowed and silent head.

The confrontation ended abruptly with Richard Marlow storming off the set, past the breathless onlookers, and slamming into the small caravan—set aside from the rest—with a force that set the vehicle rocking on its wheels.

'Coffee break, everyone. Fifteen minutes,' Dean Jacobs

called cheerfully, and the frozen stillness was immediately broken with chatter and laughter.

'That's five bucks you owe me, Mira.'

Joanna watched with a frown as Mira Hobbs, the 'gofer' who had picked she and Becky up from the airport, forked over the money to Joe Kale, who was playing Becky's stern, hard-working farmer father in the movie. Joe grinned at her expression.

'Don't worry, Joanna, we're not making money out of misery.' He waved a hand to where Toni was smilingly collecting two cups of coffee and some biscuits from the catering table, and bearing them off to the enraged director's lair.

'You gotta roll with the punches in this business, kid,' Joe was telling a rather wide-eyed, unnerved Becky, 'and remember that some of the punches are feints. See, when he does this——' he pinched his nose, '——we all know what's coming.'

'It's his high sign,' Mira chipped in. 'When Richard's built up a head of steam and wants to let loose he gets Toni or Dean to oblige with an excuse. It's supposed to be a big secret but, hell, no one can keep secrets on a film set.'

'It's all sound and fury,' Joe shrugged, as he sipped his coffee. 'Better than picking up on somebody's honest mistake and blasting hell out of them.'

'And we can admire that magnificent temperament from the safety of the sidelines,' Mira laughed, slinging a spare blanket around her shoulders. The wind, sweeping down from the snows of Mount Egmont in the background, was just as bitter as she had promised when warning them at the hotel to dress up warmly.

'Richard!' As if it was a cue, Joanna heard her niece squeal.

'Hello, darling.' The man who came out of the van was smiling, relaxed, as if his temper was never anything but perfectly sweet. He kissed Becky warmly on both cheeks, responding to her impulsive hug. He was dressed in the

faded jeans, skivvy and padded jacket that seemed to be the
crew uniform and yet, like Finn Tracey, he projected an
aura of vitality that transended the physical. 'Mira look
after you OK?'

'Yes ... Oh, Richard, it's marvellous, I'm so excited!'

'It shows.' He drew a gentle hand across her flushed
cheek. 'That's partly why I wanted you down here a few
days before you're needed. I want you to have time to get
used to all of this, so that when you get before the cameras
you'll be completely at ease in the technical environment.'

Becky gave him a brilliantly grateful smile, then wound
her arm through Richard's and tugged him over to the
chairs from whence she'd sprung. 'Come and meet my aunt,
she's been *so* looking forward to meeting you. Joanna, this is
Richard Marlow.'

An unnecessary introduction if ever there was one,
Joanna thought ironically, as she met the surprised green
gaze, hiding her nervousness behind a brief smile. And did
Becky have to sound as if Joanna had been waiting all her
life for this moment?

'Welcome to the production, Joanna. I've been looking
forward to meeting you, too. Sorry we missed each other at
the school.' The liquid voice poured into her ears as he
looked her track-suited body over, from the tips of her
canvas sneakers to the blue woollen hat rolled warmly
down over her ears. He held out his hand and Joanna felt a
jolt as they touched, remembering that the last time he had
touched her it had been with his mouth. She blinked, her
hazel eyes shimmering from the slight sting of cold air
against her contact lenses.

The surprise, and the slight amusement which had been
the reaction of each member of the cast and crew she had
been introduced to, was replaced by puzzlement. 'Have we
met before?'

Joanna swallowed. Not here, not now, she thought, but
was saved from immediate reply by an exaggerated Irish
drawl.

'God, Richard, that's a hoary old line. Can't you come up with anything more original?' Finn Tracey joined them, a coat draped over his shabby costume. The two men measured unsmiling glances before Joanna found herself looking into flirting black eyes. 'You must excuse our *esteemed* director his confusion, but you see, Dean had described you as a great, strapping female, all bun and brogues!'

The unrepentant culprit admitted it beguilingly. 'I thought you'd be a nice surprise for Richard,' he told Joanna. 'Richard likes surprises.'

'He forgets I prefer to give rather than to receive, but in this case it's a pleasure,' Richard Marlow said smoothly, not taking his searching gaze off Joanna's wary face. She wished he would let go of her hand, but instead he caught up the other with an exclamation of concern.

'Good God, your hands are freezing! Didn't Mira tell you to bring gloves?'

'I forgot to pack any,' Joanna confessed, conscious of Becky moving restlessly beside her inattentive hero.

'There's a spare pair of mine in the van—Mira, would you get them? They should fit you, we're about the same size.' To her embarrassment, he matched their palms. She knew she had long hands and feet, did he have to point it out in public?

Finn was laughing as he lit up a cigarette. 'And what big hands you have, Grandma ... all the better to——'

'Shut up, Finn.' There was a definite edge to Richard's voice, and Joanna flushed with annoyance. It was his own fault ... he had practically set them up for an off-colour remark! She frowned at him.

An arrested expression came over his face. He dropped her hands, but only so that he could whisk off her blue hat. Her hair stood briefly to attention in silver ruffled tufts before sinking to follow the contour of her skull.

A familiar look of dawning delight spread across the handsome features.

'Well, well, well . . . I thought I recognised that blush—that glare. If it isn't the little owl from the première!'

The adjective niggled. 'I'm not little at all,' she pointed out stiffly. 'I'm actually above average height for a woman.' Just. She didn't dispute the owl. Making rude remarks about other people's physical shortcomings just showed his own insensitivity. At least she wasn't wearing her glasses now.

'Funny, you don't look it. It must be those bird bones.' He leaned consideringly on his stick as he ran his gaze over her once more. When he reached her chest, padded by several layers of clothing under the blue track-suit top, he grinned afresh. 'No wonder I didn't recognise you at first . . . the owl is disguised as a pouter pigeon.'

'You, on the other hand, weren't at all difficult to recognise,' she snapped, resisting the urge to cross her hands over her breasts. 'Still making an exhibition of yourself.'

'Yes, ma'am,' his meekness warned her, 'and you're still watching me, too.'

'You mean you two *have* met before?' Becky looked accusingly at her aunt, whose normally well trained temper was hanging by a thread.

'Only across a crowded room: "She was a phantom of delight. When first she gleamed upon my sight".' The beautiful voice taunted her, and Joanna realised that he was enjoying himself. The thread snapped.

'Why, Richard,' she murmured with the mild, regretful reproach that was such a powerful weapon in the classroom, 'surely you haven't forgotten everything else? Are your words and kisses *so* lightly given?"

'What?' A wary look shot into the green eyes, and the teasing smile on his lips wavered.

'And to think I was treasuring the memory of our time together,' Joanna sighed, unable to help herself now she was into a role. Richard spun on his Assistant Director.

'Dean? Is this——?'

Dean held up his hands. 'None of my doing. I didn't even

know you'd laid eyes on each other.'

'Well, actually, I shouldn't hold your defective memory against you,' Joanna said, with malicious kindness. 'You weren't too steady on your feet at the time.'

Finn Tracey gave a yelp of laughter. 'On the booze were you, Richard, you hypocrite? Too bombed to remember your sins?'

'It can't have been that night, and I'm damned sure that I'd remember if we had ever met before . . . or since.' Green eyes tried to strip Joanna's soul bare, and she felt a nip of regret at ever opening her mouth. 'As far as I know I've never had a blackout in my life.'

'We never did introduce ourselves,' she said placatingly, before she realised how it would sound.

'Oh, God, he really must be slipping.' Finn wasn't letting an opportunity to twist the knife pass by. 'Richard usually observes at least the minimal courtesies with women, don't you, old chum? Do tell, darling—did he thoroughly disgrace himself?'

'Well?' Richard murmured, ruefully conceding her victory after a moment's loaded silence. 'Are you going to enlighten us?'

'No,' said Joanna starkly, having lost her nerve entirely. The slow appreciative smile reappeared and Joanna realised, aghast, that he thought she was being provocative.

'Ah, well, I'm sure it will come to me,' he said softly.

'I hope not,' slipped out fervently. Why had she tried to taunt him with something that would really only be an embarrassment to herself?

'Really? Now you've really whetted my appetite. I adore puzzles.' Already scrambling in mental retreat, Joanna was relieved when he transferred his piercing gaze back to an eager Becky.

'Now you look after yourself, darling. I can't have my leading lady catching a cold, so don't hang around if it gets any more overcast. And if you have any questions just ask, you're surrounded by old pros who'll be happy to share their experience. Or save them up for me ... I want to continue the coaching sessions we started in Auckland. I know Joanna——' he made her sound like a life-long friend just by using her name, '——will need you for three or four hours a day on lessons, but we can work around that. How are you going with those exercises I showed you?'

'They're really helping.' Becky's eyes brimmed with enthusiasm. The intensive, one-to-one coaching sessions had been another bone that Ellen had gnawed at. 'Why is she so vague about what they do for hours and hours alone together? Sometimes she doesn't even take her script!' Ellen had cried. 'She says he's teaching her to relax and relate. What does *that* mean, I ask you?' Since Ellen's inquisitional techniques were enough to make Joanna defensively vague herself about anything from her class's pass rate to the last time she had a haircut, she could understand Becky's reluctance. Once Ellen had made up her mind about something it was almost impossible to change it, so why lay oneself open to lectures?

'I know all my lines,' Becky said proudly. 'In fact, I think I know every line in the film!'

'Ah, to be young and eager again.' Richard included Joanna in his mock sigh.

'I *am* still young,' she riposted smugly.

'You're not old,' Becky chided him, revealing her youth by taking him seriously. 'You're the perfect age.'

For what? Or rather, for whom? Joanna thought wryly.

'Thank you, darling, for your flattery,' Richard replied lightly and, catching the fleeting disdain on her aunt's face, 'What about you, Joanna, do you think I'm the perfect age?'

'You and Peter Pan,' she said crisply. His ego could look after itself.

'What a coincidence!' said the sly temptation of his smile. 'I once had the same thought about you. My personality and your ... er ... physical resemblance.'

Joanna wrestled with the strong urge to give him another

whack on the shins. 'I spend most of my working life among adolescents. Boyishness is not a trait I find endearing in a full-grown man.'

'Nor I in a woman . . .' he leaned forward to take the hat out of her hands and pull it down over her silver head, '. . . until now.' The for-her-ears-only whisper was accompanied by a sultry look that was an exact imitation of Finn Tracey's trade mark. An angry desire to giggle made Joanna's eyes sparkle furiously at him as he grinned and patted Becky lightly on the cheek before he limped away to call the end of the break.

Finn discarded his cigarette to follow. 'At least you've put him back into a good mood, lady. Let's get together some time, and you can tell me all the juicy details of your story.'

There go two very arrogant young men, Joanna thought with reluctant amusement, wondering why Finn's sexy smile had had less effect than its mocking imitation. Not that Finn was so young any more, he was in his mid-thirties, and beginning to look attractively jaded.

Magically, the atmosphere of frustration on the set had disappeared and there were no more blow-ups for the rest of the afternoon. The filming was still progressing smoothly when Joanna finally managed to persuade Becky to go back to the hotel. The half-hour drive from the farm location back to New Plymouth was accomplished at Mira's apparently usual breathless pace, and she merely dropped them at the door before heading away again with two minor character players with late afternoon calls.

The large twin-bedded suite, which Joanna and Becky shared, was on the upper of the two floors reserved for the film company, and looked out over a well-developed park. In spite of being something of an industrial 'boom town' with the advent of oil and natural gas exploration, New Plymouth still clung firmly to its agricultural roots, priding itself on its city parks and gardens. Dominated by the famous outline of Mount Egmont, it was also a tourist centre, especially during the winter ski season—at present at its height.

Harnessing Becky's excited energy, Joanna eased her into the first set of lessons with English. Becky was delighted to discover that it involved a project based on the film.

'This will be much more fun than essays,' she said cheerfully, so Joanna decided not to point out that they *were* essays, only they happened to be on a subject very dear to her heart. Becky went to an exclusive girls' school which Joanna knew was very old-fashioned in its approach to lessons. Natural ability enabled Becky to drift through the syllabus, but she was inclined to be lazy. If she was to pass her bursary exams in a few months, Joanna knew she would have to make Becky's lessons as stimulating as this new filming experience.

'What was all that between you and Richard?' Becky asked as she picked up her pen, zeroing in on a subject that Joanna had thought, and hoped, she had forgotten. 'You didn't tell me you knew him? Was it just a joke?'

'I got his autograph once,' Joanna said, choosing her words carefully to make it sound very light and meaningless. Becky's blue eyes held a possessive curiosity that she didn't intend to provoke any further. 'And you know how actors throw kisses around.'

'Yes, they do, don't they?' Satisfied, Becky continued airily, 'I rather like it . . . it's so free and open and honest the way they treat each other. They don't try to hide their feelings.'

Oh, my dear innocent, you have a lot to learn! thought Joanna with an inward grimace. Actors were the worst of the lot when it came to deception, and the most skilful. She'd had her own heart bruised fairly severely at University, before she learned that the 'frank and free relationships' among her fellows in the drama group actually meant 'casual and careless'. In a contest of chastity versus popularity, there was only one option as far as

Joanna was concerned; she cared too much about herself to feel comfortable with the constant backstage game-playing.

At seven-thirty, they went down to the plush hotel dining-room, where Mira met them at the door and led them over to one of the long tables. In a loud voice she introduced Joanna and told her to sit where she liked.

'I won't bother to name everyone, you'd probably forget them all anyway,' she said, sliding into a chair.

'Pull up a chair here, Joanna ... Becky,' the brassy blonde across the table directed. 'It's all crew down that end, and their shop talk's even more boring than ours. I'm Suzy Layton, by the way, the local tart—in the film,' she added, with an attractive laugh when Joanna looked startled. 'I actually specialise in freshly scrubbed *ingenues* but at last I've found a director willing to cast me against type. When I auditioned I told Richard that inside this sweet façade beat a heart of pure tramp and, thank God, he believed me. I'm having enormous fun being a bad girl.'

'And I'm Kelly Foster,' said the thin, middle-aged woman next to her, familiar from her role as Richard Marlow's housekeeper in the successful television detective series which had first made his name on screen. 'I'm Helen's aunt, and how I wish Richard would believe *I* was a tramp.' She gave a salacious wink that was so audacious in the lined, motherly face that Joanna giggled.

'Oh, he believed,' Suzy complained amidst laughter, 'but unfortunately, he never did ask for proof.'

Becky, whose eyes had been darting around the other tables as she hovered reluctantly before the chair beside Joanna, said, 'Aren't they back yet?'

'Half an hour ago,' said Mira, starting on the soup which was being delivered in steaming bowls. 'Otherwise yours truly would still be running around like a chicken with her head cut off. Richard had a meet with Mal—Malcolm Connelly, the scriptwriter,' she tacked on for Joanna's benefit.

'Oh God,' Joe Kale groaned from half-way down the table. 'If that means another re-write for tomorrow, I think I'm going to jump out my window.'

'Lucky you're on the ground floor, then, isn't it?' grinned Suzy. 'I'll come and do the lines with you if you like . . . that is, if your sister doesn't mind?' She threw the question at Kelly.

'Be my guest, dearie,' Kelly said. 'It's boring enough being related to him on film without having to put up with him the rest of the time.'

A rude raspberry was her reply, and as the noisy meal progressed Joanna found herself infected by the light-hearted atmosphere. It was mostly shop talk, as Suzy had predicted, with lots of outrageous gossip thrown in which Joanna took with a healthy dose of salt. Becky was lapping it up, not even seeming to mind when it was sometimes obvious that she was being teased.

Prompted finally by her charge's valiantly concealed yawns, Joanna was about to suggest they call it a night when suddenly the yawns vanished. Richard had arrived, and he announced to a chorus of groans that changes to the next day's schedule were being typed up and would be delivered to their rooms.

'Script changes, ditto, but you can stop making a noose of that napkin, Joe, because they don't include you.'

He hooked a nearby chair with his stick, and dragged it over to nudge it neatly between Joanna and Becky, who eagerly made room for him. As if by magic, a waitress appeared by his side with a steak and salad.

'Thanks, angel, I knew you wouldn't let me down,' he said with a husky gratitude that made the girl blush. 'Do you think you could do me a favour and send something up to my room? I know it's a lot to ask when you're about to finish up for the night, but there's a writer, a production assistant and an assistant director in there who could really do with an injection of energy.'

The waitress melted completely under his coaxing smile.

'I'll see what I can do,' she said breathlessly, and rushed away.

'Look at the size of this thing!' Richard looked at his still sizzling steak. 'I'll be lucky if I can get through half of it, even with my appetite.'

'You'd better heave some Joanna's way,' Mira grinned. 'I thought that *you* could put it away, but you should see *her* technique.'

Joanna knew that it was a sign of acceptance that she was being included in the friendly insults. She smiled ruefully as Kelly picked up the cue.

'She's sure going to take a bite out of the catering budget. But where does it all go, thin air? I put on a kilo just watching her.'

Joanna's eyes flicked sideways to meet Richard's amused glitter. 'Well, what's your secret, Joanna?'

Did she imagine the underlying emphasis? 'Greed,' she admitted.

'Oh, goody,' he said, in a soft voice of suggestive innocence. 'A greedy woman.'

She felt her face warm as he turned to his steak. The tousled red hair was damp, and he brought a clean, fresh aroma with him into the now smoke-laden air of the restaurant. Even though it was obvious from his slowed movements that he was tired, he had taken the trouble to shower and shave and put on a fresh shirt and black jeans.

'Sorry about not being able to make time for you today, Becky,' he told the girl who was watching him eat with dreamy eyes that Joanna was incredulously aware held a hint of maternal concern. If he didn't get them with the playboy charm, he got them by playing on the female response to vulnerability. He couldn't lose!

'But I'll make sure that from now on I set aside at least an hour in the evenings, OK? After dinner, depending on how long my post-shoot production meetings drag on. You don't have any objection to that, do you, Joanna?'

'As long as it's not too late,' Joanna said firmly.

'You needn't worry about my depriving her of her beauty sleep . . . I don't want circles under her eyes. The camera picks up tiresome little details like that all too well. Self-discipline is the secret of every screen lovely. Speaking of which, did anyone see Finn this evening?'

'He didn't come in to dinner,' Mira answered. 'He must have ordered something in his room.'

Richard's lack of expression made Joanna wonder what strong emotion he was hiding. 'Make sure he gets those changes, would you, Mira? I don't want him claiming that he wasn't told. Hand them to him *personally*, don't just slip them under the door.'

Mira slipped away as the talk became general again, and when Richard finished his steak he joined in with a wit and energy that Joanna could only admire, having it on Mira's authority that he had been up since dawn preparing for the day's shoot. Several times he tried to draw Joanna into the discussion but she resisted, preferring to observe his chameleon-like personality, and particularly his attitude to Becky. At one stage, her niece put her hand on his arm and he took her hand in his and played with it absently as he spoke. He was obviously one of those people who touched as naturally as he breathed, and Joanna could tell from his abstraction that he wasn't even aware of what he was doing. But Becky certainly was.

Deciding it was time for a tactical withdrawal, Joanna opened her mouth to suggest they join the straggling exodus from the tables, when Richard suddenly leaned back in his chair and stretched, loosening his hand from Becky's to rub a shoulder. He turned his head, caught the determination on Joanna's face, and drawled suddenly to Becky.

'Becky, darling, would you mind very much going and getting my jacket from my room? It's 218. There are some notes I made today in the inside pocket and I want to talk them over with Jeff.' He nodded to the Director of Photography at an adjacent table, sketching something on a napkin for his frowning companion. 'I'm so bushed I don't think I can take an unnecessary step, or even a necessary one.'

His stick clattered to the floor to punctuate his weary remark, and Becky leapt to pick it up. She didn't seem to notice that the smile he gave her was a replica of the coaxing one he had given to the biddable waitress.

He waited until Becky's youthful bounce had carried her out of the restaurant before turning in his chair.

'Alone at last,' he said, transferring the smile to Joanna.

'You call this alone?' she asked drily, looking around the quarter-full table. Other residents of the hotel seemed to be lingering over-long with their coffees, casting surreptitious glances at the famous man in their midst.

'You do in this business.' Richard's mouth took on a bitter-sweet tilt. 'I suppose I've learned to just block the attention out.'

'Fiddlesticks!' Joanna was unimpressed by the pathos adopted for her benefit. 'You thrive on an audience.'

'Fiddlesticks?' he murmured, delighted by the old-fashioned term. Then he admitted, unabashed, 'Most of the time I don't mind an audience, but there are times when I *revere* privacy.' He leaned the hard sweep of jaw on a slender hand, bringing the warmth and scent of him too close for comfort. His eyes locked with hers, his voice filled with a seductive quietness.

'I'm not Becky, Richard Marlow, to be impressed by a glib line of dialogue and a fine pair of eyes,' she said, trying to dissipate the spurious intimacy that he had deliberately created by moving into her personal space. She inched her chair back.

'How very Jane Austen.' He tucked his little finger into the corner of his mouth, a curving sweep that joined his eyes in laughing at her.

'I *am* an English teacher,' she pointed out. 'And Jane Austen happens to be a favourite of mine.'

'Mmm. Becky says that you teach a special class of slow learners,' he murmured with lazy interest.

'Some of them are extremely bright, they just don't happen to fit in with a disciplined school environment.' Joanna's defensiveness was automatic. Certainly, most of the pupils in her home-room class were just marking time until they were legally able to leave school, but she considered it a privilege and a challenge to try and channel their disruptive energy into constructive effort. She waited for the typical come-back, the kind of subtle intellectual snobbery that presumed a person was a failure because he or she didn't measure up to formal outdated standards of education.

'Do you do it well?' he disconcerted her by asking.

'Extremely well,' she told him challengingly.

'See? You have an ego, too,' he teasingly revealed his knowledge of her opinion of him. 'Though not as big as mine, I'll grant you. I do what I do *supremely* well.'

She laughed, as he meant her to. 'You have a nice laugh, Joanna, I like to hear it. Why were you at the première that night? Spying on us?'

'I could hardly *not* notice you, could I?' she said tartly. 'And, as it happened, I still wasn't sure at the time whether I was going to chaperon Becky.' Making it sound like the kind of offer she had every day.

'Your sister was.'

'Ellen is always sure about everything.'

'And she's used to being a centre of attention, I know; and now she finds the spotlight on her beautiful, almost grown-up daughter, while she's firmly thrust back into the role of mother,' he said with a perspicacity that was uncannily accurate. 'I realise that she might have put you in an awkward position.'

'Not at all,' Joanna said loyally. 'It's quite natural she should worry about Becky—she's never been away from home for any length of time before.' *Especially with a rich, handsome movie director offering her stardom on a plate* remained unsaid, but from the twitch of his mouth she suspected that Richard was reading her mind. 'As for the première,

Duncan and I were going anyway.'

As a diversion it was overly successful. 'Oh yes, the headmaster with the freckles,' he murmured. 'Do they have casting couches, too, in the educational department?'

'No, they have canes,' said Joanna crisply. 'To use on little boys who think that toilet-wall crudity is the height of wit.'

There was a small, startled silence, then Richard made a graceful gesture of apology with his expressive hands. 'I'm sorry, Joanna, sometimes I forget where I am. For a while I lived in the kind of fast lane where bad taste is considered sophisticated. Forgive me.'

Joanna was having none of the charming sincerity. 'I'm so glad to see that you haven't entirely given up acting— you're very good at it, you know.'

His complacency frowned at her irony. 'Please, Joanna. I have apologised.'

'And are your apologies always accepted without question?' she asked drily.

He looked at her, then shrugged with cynical resignation. 'Invariably.'

'Then, of course I accept,' she said casually, as if it was of no consequence at all, and had the pleasure of seeing him momentarily speechless. He had been expecting her to enjoy making him grovel.

This time the green glitter in his eyes was wholly unrehearsed. 'You b——' He caught himself and laughed. '"She was a vixen when she went to school: And though she be but little, she is fierce".'

'I told you before, I'm not little. And you're mixing your metaphors, Shakespeare notwithstanding. I thought I was an owl.'

'I know, I think I need a good English teacher to whip me into shape. Do you know any, offhand?'

'None who are available, no.' The exhilarating banter was getting dangerous.

'Oh? It's serious then, with you and Freckles?'

'*Duncan* and I may get engaged, yes,' she said with dignity.

'May? Ah, well, there's many a slip ...'

'You should know.' Damn—what made her say something so cruel?

'Oh, I do, believe me, I do.' Showing no sign of being crushed by her oblique reference to Bianca James. 'And in my experience it's always wise to have a friend close by to point out the pitfalls.'

'We're not friends. I only met you today.'

'So!' He pounced triumphantly. 'That *was* only a put-up job this afternoon! We haven't met before.' He looked so thoroughly pleased with himself that Joanna pricked his bubble with pleasure.

'I meant we were only *introduced* today.' She should have known what all the soft-soaping was about. He had been acting all along, and she was furious with herself for feeling faintly disappointed.

'We actually kissed?' His eyes narrowed disconcertingly on her mouth.

'Yes.'

'You're sure it was me?'

'Unless there's someone else going around signing himself—all my love, Richard.'

'Signing? I wrote you a *note*?' He sounded appalled, and Joanna lowered her lashes to hide the mischief in her eyes. It was delicious to be able to dangle him on a string ... he looked so dismayed at the idea of having committed a casual indiscretion to paper.

'Yes ... and we talked about your work ...' she hoped the laughter in her voice might be mistaken for a broken-hearted sob, '... we shared so much ... and I really thought that you ... oh!' Her chin had been taken in a steely grasp and lifted sharply. Her trembling laughter was revealed.

'You little devil,' he breathed in amused threat. 'How much of this is——?' He blinked suddenly and let her chin go, leaving a tingling warmth where his fingers had lain along the bone. 'Damn it, here comes our chaperon again.' He had seen Becky out of the corner of his eye.

Our chaperon? The role reversal had all sorts of dangerous implications and Joanna, who had been blind to everything but Richard, caught her breath as he promised softly, 'Don't think I'm letting you get away with this. Do you know the cardinal rule of movie-making? Always give the director what he wants! I have a feeling, my not-so-little owl, that what this director is going to want is—*you*!'

CHAPTER THREE

'ONLY been here four days and already you're bored to sleep?'

Joanna's eyes fluttered open to see Richard Marlow leaning on the corner of the caravan which protected the row of folding canvas chairs from the wind.

'I'm not bored.' She yawned, the hot dryness of her lenses telling her that she had indeed fallen asleep. 'Cold, tired and uncomfortable, but not bored. I've never been bored in my life.'

'Just the novelty wearing off, mmm?' Joanna watched Richard take one of the canvas chairs next to her and stretch out his bad leg, tapping his stick absently against his thigh as he leaned back gratefully. The scenes this morning required only Becky, Finn and John Marker, who was playing Michael. Consequently, there were few of the usual hangers-on about, and Joanna had been left mostly to her own devices during the long stretch of camera rehearsals. She blinked rapidly, trying to lubricate her lenses. They constantly caused her problems, but it irked her to think that she could be beaten by something less than the size of a finger-nail, so she persevered in wearing them. Mind over matter, she assured herself, as the blessed moistness filmed over the tiny scraps of porous plastic.

'Are you flirting with me?'

'My contact lenses are irritating me.' Rather like you, her chilly stare declared. He looked so wretchedly good-looking, dressed from neck to toe in black, a dramatic contrast to the white skin and red hair. Unlike everyone else, he never wore a hat, even on the coldest days. Perhaps the flames on his head kept him warm, or perhaps he just knew what a dramatic picture he presented bareheaded, she thought sourly.

'Poor darling,' he commiserated. 'Why don't you take them out and give your eyes a rest?'

My sentiments exactly, she thought, glowering at him. She was loath to let on exactly how blind she was without her visual aids; it made her feel too vulnerable. She had the feeling that around this man she would have to be very strong if she wasn't going to succumb to his undoubted attractions. Besides, it would be just one more thing for him to tease her about . . . and he needed no more assistance on that score.

'Actually,' he continued, enjoying her glare, 'I think I like you better in spectacles . . . they sort of balance your face.'

'Over-balance, you mean. I suppose you think I should be flattered at being likened to an owl.'

'Why not? Owls are darlings,' he told her, tiny lines fanning at the corners of his smiling eyes. They'll be the size of tram-lines by the time he's forty, thought Joanna with snide resignation . . . and he'll still be handsome! 'Owls are strange and lovely, mystical creatures who haunt the night with their magical presence . . . rather the way you haunt my nights.'

The blatant untruth made Joanna acerbic. 'They can give you a nasty peck, too, if you try and mess with them. There's nothing mystical about owls, that's just human superstition.'

'What a terribly prosaic woman you are,' he sighed.

'Yes, I am, aren't I?' said Joanna, pleased that he realised it. She wasn't one of his actress friends, willing to play meaningless games to while away a few moments of his spare time. She had her feet firmly on the ground.

'Except when you're asleep.' He leaned over and casually tucked the tartan rug she had commandeered for her own, more securely over her legs. 'When you're asleep you look whimsical, and when you wake up and blink those big, sleepy-soft brown eyes at me, you look quite deliciously cute.'

'It's your fault I'm sleepy,' Joanna grumbled. She knew she wasn't beautiful, but 'cute' relegated her to adolescent ranks. 'Becky kept me up half the night going over lines that she's known off by heart for weeks, simply because you murmured that you might change the emphasis at last night's coaching session. And then I get dragged out of bed this morning for a *dawn* make-up call.'

'Best part of the day,' he said blithely.

'I thought you were a night person.'

'Owl,' he said with a grin. 'What makes you say that?'

'I hear you thumping about at all hours.' She had not been entirely happy to discover their room was right next to Richard's, especially since Becky seemed to be constantly thinking up excuses to 'pop next door to ask Richard something'. And he always welcomed her, however busy he happened to be.

'I had no idea the walls were that thin.'

'They're not, you just make a hell of a racket.'

'I thought I was being very quiet. Are you sure you don't lie there with your ear pressed to the wall?'

'My bed is over by the window.' Her quelling look had no effect.

'Pity,' his eyebrows raised and lowered lecherously, 'and there I was, imagining I only had to turn over and you were practically in my arms!'

'Would you know the difference?' she asked acidly, to

cover a minor tremor. No doubt he had had hundreds of women in his arms.

'Between you and the wall?' He purposely chose to misunderstand. He looked at the shapeless hump of the blanket and cocked his head. 'Sure I would—the wall is taller than you.'

She almost laughed with him. 'And more receptive than I'll ever be.'

'Don't you mean *responsive*?' He was delighted to take advantage of her slip, golden flecks radiating through the laughing green eyes. 'Or are you suggesting that I'm so frustrated that I have to vent my passions——'

'*Richard!*' Joanna felt the glow spread through her entire body as she wriggled under the blanket in embarrassment. 'Stop it! Of course I'm not . . . I mean . . . I'm sure you have plenty . . . oh, for goodness sake, stop *laughing*!' She watched him shaking in the chair, torn between the desire to shake him and the almost equal desire to join him. 'For all I care, you can have orgies every night!' she cried in exasperation, wondering how the conversation had strayed so far. 'As long as you don't keep me awake.'

'Why, Joanna, is that a bit of the green-eyed monster peeping out?' he conquered his laughter to ask, impishly.

'The only green-eyed monster around here is *you*,' she told him.

'Surely I'm not that bad?' he said, amusement spun with lightning dexterity into hurt.

'"Mad, bad, and dangerous to know",' she said severely, then was annoyed at herself for slipping into his own irritating habit of sprinkling his conversation with unnervingly appropriate quotations.

'You think I'm Byronesque?' He looked disgustingly flattered.

'*Finn* is Byronesque,' she said, knowing it would annoy him. She hadn't worked out yet whether the two men were still friends or enemies. There was certainly conflict between them, both on and off the set. 'With hair that colour you don't really fit the bill. In fact, if I half close my eyes——' she did so to hide the vengeful humour, '——I would say that you had the perfect colour scheme to be a Muppet.'

His pique was brief. Though he was capable of temperamental fireworks, Joanna noticed that he didn't sulk afterwards . . . or brood like Finn. He shrugged off his temper and went back to work, no hard feelings. That was why, she realised with surprise, that she felt safe when she gave in to the urge to annoy him. He didn't bear grudges and he respected people who stood up to him, even as he was ripping their heads off!

'If we're going to get personal about hair, darling, you'd better look to that crew-cut of yours.'

'It's a razor-cut!' she snapped.

'Who did the colouring?'

'God.'

'You mean it's natural?' He was curious now, rather than amused. 'Then how come your brows and lashes are dark?'

'*They're* tinted. I can't wear make-up with my lenses,' she said reluctantly, sensing that part of his curiosity was professional. He had had some very firm opinions about Becky's film make-up, and had even given her a lecture about what cosmetics to wear off-screen.

'Mmm . . .' He seemed to go off into a dream, staring at her. Then his eyes slowly wandered down the tartan. The illicit thought popped into her head that he was wondering if she tinted the rest of her body hair, too, and she went scarlet at the thought. Her hands actually went clammy imagining the kind of circumstances in which he might find out. She vividly remembered a scene from one of his films where he and Bianca James were in a semi-darkened room, city lights shining through the blinds to stripe the dull gleam of their bodies. He had been a beautiful lover in a scene both explicit and discreet.

'What are you thinking about?'

'What?' She shifted abruptly, nearly collapsing the

chair. 'Nothing, why?'

'You're blushing.'

'Am I?' She felt her hot cheek, avoiding his eyes. 'It's the cold, that's all.'

'If you say so,' he said, with such wicked blandness that she wondered nervously if her unruly thoughts had been transparent. Richard was used to reading facial expressions, could he read hers?

'How did Becky do this morning?' She changed the subject firmly. 'She was rather disappointed that you didn't say much about yesterday.'

'First day in front of the cameras is always difficult, even for the professionals. She did well enough. I can't be more specific than that until I see the rushes and, since they have to go up to Auckland to be processed, we won't be able to see them until tomorrow evening at the earliest.'

'Well *enough*?' Joanna sat straighter, her instinct for evasion—honed by several years' experience in the classroom—alerted by his casualness. 'And is well enough good enough for *your* film? Are you always so easy to please?' He hadn't been so far. He was a perfectionist, meticulous for detail when he was at work. The technicians grumbled, but they respected him for it.

'I'll know when I see the scenes on film. It's what the camera sees that's important, not the human eye.' The evasion drew even more scorn.

'Really? What was it you said the other night: "in art, as in love, instinct is enough"? Are you telling me you *don't* have an instinct? I thought that you were supposed to be the one with the picture inside your head ... projecting your dreams through the camera, didn't you say? What kind of director is it who doesn't know what he's doing until he sees it on film?'

'What do you want me to say?' he asked, with a wry awareness of being trapped by his own words. 'That she's terrible?'

'Is she?'

'At the moment—yes.' His direct simplicity was a challenge.

'Have you told her that?' Joanna demanded, aghast.

'Of course I haven't, what the hell do you take me for?' he said with violent annoyance. 'Look, Joanna, it's only to be expected that she's going to be stiff and self-conscious. Why do you think I'm starting her off with these very minor scenes? . . . because they're ones I can work around if need be. The important thing is for her to relax, to be natural. She's not an actress and I haven't got time to turn her into one; I have to draw on her natural feelings and instincts, and work very closely with her to establish her confidence in herself and in me.'

'Oh, she has the utmost confidence in you,' Joanna said, drily. Becky had been his shadow for the past four days, delighted by any crumb of his attention.

'At least allow that I know what I'm doing, Joanna.'

'Do you?' she murmured, not thinking about the film, or Becky's part in it, but Becky herself.

'You must have an opinion.' Richard's mind was squarely on his film. 'What did you think of *Foreign Tongues*?' It was the first film he had directed. 'Did you like the way I handled that?'

'I don't know, I haven't seen it,' she admitted brazenly. His outrage was beautifully done, and she was urged to mischief. 'And I'm not an official member of your fan club, although I do boast a sample of your autograph.'

His response to her teasing was instant. His voice was all light and innocence, banishing the previous undertone of seriousness. 'So you do . . . tell me again how I came to give it to you . . .?'

'I haven't told you the first time, yet.' Joanna could be as innocent as he. 'Besides, I know how famous people *revere* their private moments. I couldn't possibly kiss-and-tell.'

'How refreshing, most of the women I know seem to take it for granted that a kiss will make the papers, preferably with photos.' He slanted her a sly look. 'You can trust me

... I'll be as close as the grave.'

'What a coincidence.' Joanna spoke coolly to his dancing eyes. 'That's the exact phrase Toni used when she asked me about it yesterday. And when *he* asked, Dean said that the grave was a blabbermouth compared to him. I don't suppose that you put them up to wheedling it out of me, did you?'

'Who? *Moi?*' He looked so pained that she laughed. 'My dear young woman, would I be so devious?'

'Yes.'

'You know there are bets riding on this . . . about how we met?'

'No!' Joanna put a gloved hand over her heart, eyes widening in exaggerated astonishment. Betting, along with running card and chess games, topped the list as a way to pass the long hours spent hanging around, awaiting the moment when the cameras would roll for a few more minutes. Cast and crew alike were addicted. 'If you really want to know, you could try asking Becky.'

'She knows?' His mouth drooped with a vague disappointment that Joanna found very satisfying.

'The expurgated version,' she said smugly, and he brightened.

'That's no good to me, I don't believe in bowdlerizing a classic story. I'll wait until the original comes out. Anyway,' the white lids sank over an impossibly sexy look, 'it would spoil the fun of trying to find out.'

'And of course, you must have your fun.'

'Of course I must; I have to relax too. I work very hard.'

Joanna throttled another pert remark. Autocratic he might be, but it was also true that he worked harder than anyone on-set. Although Dean funnelled off the trivia of day-to-day organisational problems, Richard kept his fingers firmly on the pulse. And his directing was a physical affair: he coaxed, he threatened, he gentled, he bullied, he whispered, he shouted, he sweated. At times he showed an astonishing patience; at times he showed none at all. He kept a tight rein, but he seemed to know exactly the right moment to let it go slack, and to encourage the periodic bursts of idiocy and practical joking that helped defuse the energy-sapping tension of a difficult scene.

She noticed him surreptitiously rubbing his leg. 'Is it hurting?' she asked, her voice carefully devoid of pity.

'Just a little stiff,' he said, dismissively. 'It's the cold, I think.'

'You should have set the movie on a tropical island.'

'Are you kidding, on our budget?' The teasing grin became a little distant as he tipped his head back to look at the upward sweep of Egmont. 'A large part of this film *is* this landscape ... it wouldn't have worked the same anywhere else. Mal was born down here, you know, and he wanted to use the brooding threat of the bush, the mountain dwarfing everything and everyone, the mist from the sea, cold breath in the air, the damp-dark greenness of the land and the inevitability of nature ...'

In a few words, he had sketched the atmosphere of the film with eerie perfection. In the same way, he used his words and voice to create an imaginary world for his actors to inhabit, helping them to screen out the distracting reality of cameras and lights. At its most potent it was almost a form of hypnotism. His trained voice could make one believe almost anything. What was he making Becky believe? Joanna wondered. Each night she came back from her after-dinner 'session' with Richard feverishly bright-eyed and excited. Joanna couldn't bring herself to seriously entertain Ellen's confused and darkling hints about Richard Marlow's plans for her daughter—after all, this was a man who had squired about some of the most beautiful women in the world and, by his own admission, lived an extremely sophisticated life. A naïve teenager, however lovely, would scarcely interest him after the likes of Bianca James. On the other hand, if he was in the habit of casual encounters with women, he might not think twice about taking what was offered to him on a plate. If Becky carried her hero-worship a step further would he risk alienating her by rejecting her? How did his personal integrity weigh up against his artistic ambition?

Joanna had murmured something to Suzy Layton about Richard treating Becky with the casual affection of a favoured pet, and not been reassured by the response.

'That's just the way Richard is,' Suzy had said cheerfully. 'He's naturally affectionate, and when he puts his soul into things he expects others to do the same. And mostly they do. He has this incredible gift of being able to make people *want* to please him.'

'I suppose all his leading ladies used to fall in love with him,' said Joanna wryly. Perhaps there was safety for Becky in numbers.

'And vice versa.' Suzy's sunny grin sat oddly beneath the hard-faced make-up and the brassy hair which she confessed was actually a quiet shade of mouse. 'He's very hot on emotive realism, you may have noticed . . . "If you would have me weep, you must first of all feel grief yourself" . . . that type of thing. He fell in love with his romantic co-stars with clockwork regularity. Nobody bothered to even lay odds on it. Only that last time, with Bianca, did it get serious . . .' She suddenly remembered who she was gossiping to, and hastened to dismiss Joanna's faint expression of anxiety.

'Hey . . . this is all history, Joanna. I mean, if you're worrying about Becky, don't. I know she follows him, all eyes, but he's not an actor any more, he's the *director*. I doubt if he even notices her except in context of the film. He pays her a lot of attention, sure, but as I said, that's just his way, it's not necessarily indicative of *personal* interest. He knows he's attractive to women, he could hardly help it the way they throw themselves at him, but the big thing is that he actually *likes* women. A lot of male stars have this great macho thing about their reputations as studs, but they don't actually like or trust women very much—they're happier palling around with the guys. Richard has tons of women friends, he likes their companionship, though God knows, what with Bianca chucking him over and all the actresses who've tried to bed-hop their way into the movies, he has reason enough to be a little paranoid.'

Now, as she watched Richard rise and frown down towards the river where Jeff Hobbs and his crew were setting up the camera positions, Joanna acknowledged that there was something irresistibly likeable about him, quite apart from the sexual magnetism that he seemed to switch on and off at will.

'So, there you are.' Finn Tracey came upon them, sounding as if he had stumbled on a secret assignation. 'Sorry to drag you away from such delightful company, Mr Director,' he smiled sardonically at Richard, not looking sorry at all, 'but Billy says there's a problem with the river—he wants you down there.' He jerked his head down towards the action. Today they were located in an isolated part of the Mount Egmont National Park, and Billy Williams, the stunt co-ordinator, was preparing his stunt-men for a scene where Helen's brother was rescued from a flood-swollen river by David. Becky, too, was in the scene and Joanna only hoped that she could carry off her few lines better than she obviously had the day before.

'You look cosy.' The mocking black eyes turned on Joanna. 'Mind if I join you under the rug?' Joanna grinned, used by now to his boldness.

'Don't bother, Finn.' Richard forestalled his move with a curt command. 'I want you to have that make-up re-checked. We have a few extreme close-ups coming and I want Loren to make sure you're absolutely waterproof. Thanks to your decision not to answer make-up call this morning we're already running behind schedule.' Because of the complexity of Finn's make-up, he usually had to report to Loren two hours before everyone else, but he was notorious for his tardiness both on and off the set. Loren, who was an easygoing young woman, spat tacks whenever his name was mentioned, and swore she'd never work on another film with him.

Finn shrugged. 'Plenty of time, Richard. You have to sort out this problem yet.' Joanna didn't know whether his casualness was a deliberate attempt to annoy Richard or not, although Dean had told her that Finn had a reputation for being difficult to work with. 'But he delivers the goods, eventually, so he still gets chosen over more amenable actors. A headache for directors but the backers love 'im.'

'*Now*, Finn.' Normally, Richard was inclined to ignore Finn's attempts to needle him, but this time there was an edge to his voice that brooked no refusal. For a moment the two men stared at each other, and Joanna thought that Finn was going to make an issue of it. But then he shrugged, his mouth curving slyly.

'"Sits the wind in that corner?" How interesting! See you later, honey,' he said to Joanna. 'Save me a seat at lunch.'

It was purely a turn of phrase since lunch was strictly buffet, but Richard chose to further assert his authority.

'She won't be here. I want Becky back at the hotel as soon as her scenes are finished. I'm going to leave her close-ups until tomorrow, so you'd better get her quota of lessons in while you can——'

'But I've got them with me. You said we could use your cara——'

'She'll be cold and wet; you can't expect her to concentrate until she's had a hot shower or bath,' Richard pointed out, with a curt impatience that implied that he shouldn't have to do her job. Joanna was irritated by his sudden change of mood. A few minutes ago he had been flirting with her, now she was a scapegoat for his temper. 'Finn? Loren's waiting for you.'

'OK, OK.' The actor bowed to Joanna, smiling to himself rather than at her, she thought. 'He hath spoken. But maybe we can get together later, honey, at dinner. Unless, of course, Richard wants *Becky* to have an early night ...'

Behind his whistling back, Richard gave Joanna a look

that she found impossible to interpret, almost as if he blamed *her* for Finn's behaviour.

Perhaps it was the memory of that look, and her desire to thumb her nose at it, that weakened her protests that evening when Finn dragged her away from the long table to dine at his, prominent by its splendid isolation in the middle of the room. No fan would dare approach Finn without some sign of encouragement, for he was notorious for his unpredictable attitude to autograph-seekers. Even the waiters seemed nervous of his Irish temper, Joanna noticed in amusement.

'Where's that darling niece of yours ... awaiting His Lordship's pleasure?' he drawled, as he ordered for them both without asking Joanna her preference.

'I believe they were going to eat and work at the same time,' she replied calmly.

He laughed, the strong lines of his face tilting towards dissipation. 'If you believe that, you'll believe anything.'

'John is with them, too, going over tomorrow's scene.' Joanna tried not to let him see how relieved she had been to learn that. Becky had been slightly put out to discover that she was going to share one of her precious 'sessions'.

'He can't keep sparing time for you for ever,' Joanna had told her. 'Perhaps he thinks John needs a bit of assistance, too.'

'But he's already a professional.' The lovely face was disgruntled.

'But young, and anyway, in theatre you never stop learning. There's never any point when you can say that your training is finished.'

Becky laughed, her spirits shooting back up. 'Mine has only just started, I haven't even considered the finish of anything yet. Oh, I wish this film could go on and on for ever!'

Joanna had watched her with an awful feeling of inevitability. Whatever the outcome of this infatuation with Richard, Becky wasn't going to go home and meekly settle back down under her mother's thumb. She was tasting new freedoms, experimenting with new feelings and Joanna sensed a major adolescent rebellion looming. Becky was doing very well with her schoolwork, catching up on work which she had skimped on in the previous term. Joanna had no doubt that she was capable of passing her bursary exams but, if Ellen started bringing down the heavy parental hand, Becky was quite capable of throwing away her chances merely to spite her mother. In the meantime, Joanna would just have to maintain a watching brief, to ensure that all this attention didn't distort Becky's priorities, and rely on the girl's basic common sense to triumph over her love of the dramatic.

Finn didn't appear to mind Joanna's preoccupied thoughts. He embarked on a series of wicked stories about Hollywood goings-on that soon had her full attention. He was malicious, but his maliciousness had style and she couldn't help laughing at a wit which relied in part on shock for its effect. He flirted as naturally as he breathed, and she noticed that he didn't eat much of the food before him, preferring to watch in amusement as hers disappeared with its customary speed. He certainly knocked back the wine, however, and gibed when she refused more than a glass.

'Come on, it's already paid for. Or don't you have much of a head for it?' He gave her a slyly lustful look. 'In which case I must insist!'

'Actually, it's the other way around,' admitted Joanna sheepishly. 'I can drink like a fish and it doesn't affect me, so I really don't see the point.'

'God, a woman after me own heart!' Finn crowed delightedly, sweeping the black comma of hair off his forehead. 'Let's see if we can drink each other under the table.'

'No thanks, I have to set a good example for Becky.' Joanna covered the top of her glass with her hand. Finn looked rakish enough completely sober but, with a few drinks on board, he was beginning to look reckless.

'How boring for you, darling.' Finn refilled his own glass. 'Tell me, are you permanently or semi-permanently attached to anyone?'

'Sort of.' She supposed that wanting to be would count, though Duncan's warm, steadying influence seemed a long way away.

Finn laughed sourly. 'Sounds like me.'

Joanna didn't know whether he wanted her to ask the obvious question or not, so she stayed silent under his challenging stare and, after a moment, he gave her a reckless smile. 'Care to share a lonely man's bed tonight?'

'Where? Where?' she said instantly, projecting an eager excitement into her voice as she craned her neck to look around the restaurant. To her relief, Finn roared with laughter after the first stunned second, attracting curious glances from the surrounding tables. If anyone else had asked her that question, in that insolent tone of voice, she might have decked him, but she sensed that Finn's deliberate provocativeness was born out of an inner pain.

After that his flirtation took on a relaxed air of relief that told Joanna that she had passed some kind of test. His ego appeared undented by the rejection—he didn't even seem piqued—and she wondered whether his reputation as a dedicated womaniser wasn't wildly exaggerated.

The next evening, Joanna wasn't quite so accommodating when Becky again announced that she was going to eat with Richard in his room.

'You've been on-set nearly all day and busy with lessons ever since you got back. I appreciate that you're working hard, Becky, but you've got to relax, too. I think Richard could let you forgo rehearsing tonight. He must realise that you can't keep up this kind of pace for weeks on end.'

'We won't be rehearsing all the time, I'll just be keeping him company,' Becky said, a look on her face that was reminiscent of her mother's at her most determinedly self-righteous. 'He's in a production meeting right now, and I know that after everyone else leaves he'll keep right on working. He'll probably forget to eat if I'm not there to remind him.'

'I doubt he'll let himself starve to death,' Joanna commented drily. 'Then who would direct his masterpiece?'

Becky, brushing her long, golden locks into carefully tousled glory, winced at the heresy. 'He needs someone who cares about him for himself,' she said, showing disapproval of her aunt's flippancy. 'He's surrounded by people but, really, he's lonely. There are so few people that he can allow himself to be totally natural with.' Implying that she, Becky, was one of them. 'Everyone is always making demands on him, wanting things from him, he hardly ever gets any peace. They seem to forget how he's suffered. I think he needs someone just to be there, so that he doesn't brood.' She didn't seem to notice the contradictions in her confident pronouncement, so Joanna decided to gently point them out.

'Aren't you making demands on him too, wanting some of the time he's so short of? Perhaps he needs time to brood. People do, you know.'

'*I* don't make demands on him.' Becky's honey-coloured skin flushed with temper. 'If he doesn't want me there he only has to say ... but he doesn't. He likes having me around! He likes having someone to pass his experience on to. He's teaching me far more than I could ever learn going to acting lessons, and he's proud of me, he thinks I have great potential. Richard wouldn't say that unless it was true.' Her stormy-blue eyes defied Joanna to argue. 'Richard never lies about his work. He says that you have to know the truth about yourself before you can even begin to find the truth about the character that you're trying to portray. I think he gets as much out of it as I do,' she said, with the monumental arrogance of the young and beautiful. 'He's moulding and shaping my abilities with his own. He wants me to be the best, and I will be.'

Ellen would have a blue fit if she could hear her

daughter, Joanna thought, but she wisely decided not to comment further. Vowing to have a quiet talk of her own with Richard Marlow, very soon, she had let Becky flit off on her mission of mercy, while Joanna went ruefully downstairs to the restaurant to find that Finn had been waiting for her, an empty glass at his elbow and another, half-full in his hand. Even as she was entertained by his conversation, she noticed that the faintest of slurs pared his normally effortless diction and when, after dinner, he ordered another bottle of wine—this time champagne—she refused to stay and watch him empty it, softening her refusal with a joke. 'I didn't think we were on a champagne budget with this movie.'

'Gotta give Richard some problems to get his teeth into.' Finn's black eyes reproached her for her defection. 'Character building . . . he's always at his best when he's got a challenge . . . too many things been too easy for him. Especially women . . . shall I tell you about my friend Richard and his women? Shall I tell you about my friend Richard and my wife . . . my wife! It's a conspiracy, you see . . . they think I don't know . . .'

He had lapsed into dark silence and Joanna had slipped away, feeling guilty for abandoning him, but not wanting to encourage his descent into public drunkenness. She also felt guilty for her rabid curiosity. What exactly had happened in that triangle . . . and what was the conspiracy?

Her guilt reared its ugly head again the next morning, when Richard had a very character-building fit when Finn failed to arrive on set at the appointed time. They were back at the river location and had shot several scenes which didn't involve Finn, when Mira sent a message via the ranger station that she could not find their principal actor. He hadn't been waiting at the hotel when Mira had returned to collect him for his make-up call, and nobody seemed to know where he was.

Richard exploded, ending up with a few stormy remarks about the dire consequences of unprofessionalism in bit-player or star. 'Well? Where the hell is he, then?' he demanded of his captive audience. 'Did anyone see him at all this morning?'

Nobody had, and Richard's face darkened ominously. He swung the stick in his hand as if he was tempted to break a few heads. 'What about last night, then?'

Kelly threw an apologetic look at Joanna as she said slowly, 'I saw him quite late in the restaurant with Joanna.'

A slow turn was punctuated with a melodramatic raising of haughty eyebrows. Joanna felt like the accused in the dock, sure that it was exactly what he intended her to feel. 'We shared a table,' she admitted, adding defensively, 'Becky was eating with you in your room.'

'And what time did you two say goodnight?' The *if* hung heavily in the cold air and Joanna began to feel the blood heat her cheeks.

'I'm not sure——' she began, trying to swallow her anger at being treated like a criminal.

'Well, think, woman!' Richard thundered, and her temper sizzled like butter on a skillet.

'Don't you use that tone with me, mister!' she rapped, and the startled titters around them were quelled by a sweeping scowl from under lowered red brows.

'I would like to speak to you, in my caravan please, Joanna.' It was as soft and nice as pie, but an order none the less. He limped heavily as he walked away, but anger hardened her heart against the ploy. He had to duck his head to go in the door and, once inside, Joanna found that the roomy van seemed suddenly distressingly small, especially with the door closed. He only ever closed the door when he was in a temper. She braced herself.

'Damn it, are you deliberately trying to be obstructive? Because——'

'Take a deep breath.'

'*What?*' His fury mounted rather than abated, until sparks seemed to shoot from his eyes.

'Take a deep breath and count to ten. Then start again,'

Joanna said calmly. Some of her pupils were young men with quick-fire tempers, and foul mouths to match. They were also a lot taller than she was, a great deal huskier than Richard Marlow, and used to expressing anger physically. The first priority was always to calm them down. Richard didn't seem a physically violent man, but she wasn't about to be intimidated by his temper.

'Don't treat me like one of your schoolboys, Joanna——'

'Then stop throwing your weight around and trying to impress me with your lack of self-control.'

'Oh, for——' He threw his stick at the wall, and it made a satisfying thump before falling harmlessly to the floor.

'How come you never manage to hit anything—or anyone—with that thing?' Joanna remarked coolly. 'You toss it around enough in your blind rages, so I've heard. Perhaps you just have bad aim, or perhaps you're not in such a *blind* rage as you'd like everyone to think.'

'Joanna——' The lovely straight teeth were barely a millimetre apart, setting the growl back in his throat.

'I'm not responsible for Finn's behaviour.' She decided, wisely, that she'd better not annoy him any more. 'He's a grown man, he makes his own decisions. Yes, I had dinner with him last night, but left the restaurant before some of the others ... it wasn't *that* late.'

'Where did you go? To his room?' He propped himself against the table that was scattered with scripts and papers and empty coffee-cups.

'No, I did not,' she snapped back. 'Not that it's anything to do with you!'

'This is *my* film that he's sabotaging with his bloody-mindedness——' he declared savagely.

'You can't think he's deliberately trying to——'

'Can't I? You tell me, you seem to be closer to him these days than anyone else—whenever I want him he always seems to be with you.' He sneered as beautifully as he did everything else. 'Were you drinking?'

'A little.'

He snorted. 'Now *that* I know is a lie. Finn never drinks just a little.'

'You asked if *I* was drinking.' Joanna was reduced to defensive inanity.

'Stop playing word-games with me, Joanna; you know damned well what I meant.'

'And I'll say it again, I'm not his keeper. I hardly know him.'

'That doesn't stop you encouraging him.'

'*Encouraging* him?' Joanna yelled at him, her eyes spitting and sparkling.

'Giggling in corners with him. You're supposed to be chaperoning Becky, not Finn. I didn't hire you to distract my actors.'

Joanna wished she had her own stick to throw. 'I happen to like him.'

'Well, don't like him too much, darling, he's a married man. And let's not forget Freckles, waiting faithfully back home ...'

Joanna bristled furiously. 'How dare you suggest that——'

'I know Finn is damned good-looking, and that that moody, broody Irish act goes over big with women,' he said, in a kindly tone that made Joanna more furious than his outright anger, 'but I know him and, believe me, it's just an act. That's his speciality, making women fall head over heels for him; it's what makes him such a bankable proposition.'

'I thought that was your speciality,' Joanna said nastily.

His temper vanished with a suddenness that left Joanna breathless. He grinned. 'It palled.'

Joanna took a grip on herself, resisting the aggravating charm. 'Maybe for you. But what about Becky?'

His grin didn't waver, but a hint of wariness entered his eyes. 'What about Becky?'

'Don't act the innocent with me, Richard,' Joanna told him, carrying the battle squarely into his field. 'She's infatuated with you.'

He shrugged. 'All actresses fall in love with their directors ... or their leading men. Would you rather I let her fall for Finn?'

'You actually *admit* that you're playing on her emotions?' cried Joanna, appalled that he could admit so casually to fulfilling all Ellen's fears.

'I'm admitting that it was inevitable.' Richard's hands expressed a regretful truth, while the narrow face settled into such sincere lines that Joanna found herself again fighting the urge to throw caution to the winds, and agree with every word he said. 'Come on, Joanna, you must have an insight into the adolescent psyche—you said you had a degree in education. This is a brave new world to her and, like Miranda, she fell in love with her first sight of it. Why shouldn't she? A lot of us do. It's exciting, challenging and enormously satisfying when done well. What in heaven's name do you want me to do, slap Becky down? Destroy the very fragile beginnings of her confidence in herself as a woman, as well as an actress? We all need certain illusions, Joanna, even you.'

'We're talking about real life, not a play or a film.'

'Are you sure?' he asked, with a solemn sureness that undermined her own. 'Life imitates art. Are you sure that on some level Becky isn't aware that she's weaving an imaginative fantasy, one that can help her cope with reality, one that she'll probably abandon when she's more secure in herself?'

'That doesn't mean you have to weave it with her. You don't have to be quite so ... accommodating.' She glared at his grin. Why was he looking so pleased with himself? Did he think he was getting around her with his winning words? 'You're carrying on like ... like ...'

'Svengali? Swallowing up her life?'

'Exactly! Why don't you back off, let her find her own feet?'

'Because she's not ready yet.' He tilted his head and

looked at her small, agitated face gravely. 'It's the way filming works, Joanna. It swallows your life, your energy, your emotions, for weeks on end and then spews them out again for the world to admire and exclaim over and, hopefully, pay to see. We're all stuffed together into a pressure-cooker until this thing is over. We're like a family—we love, we hate, we argue, we fight, we live in each other's pockets—how could we do otherwise? Feelings are bound to get intense, they *need* to. If everything went smoothly, if we were all calm and sensible and unemotional, we'd end up with a pretty dead film on our hands.'

'There's no danger of that with you around.' Joanna was annoyed at herself for seeing his point so clearly, but her protective instincts came first. 'You love it, don't you . . . all this strife and upheaval? You're even enjoying this now . . . being in a fury.'

'Of course I am. Aren't you?'

'Oh yes, terribly,' she said sarcastically, her jaw taking on a stubborn slant that made his eyes crinkle teasingly.

'"No mask like open truth to cover lies. As to go naked is the best disguise",' he quoted softly.

'Aren't we getting away from the subject here?' Joanna said repressively, made uneasy by his habit of seeing beneath the surface.

'All right . . . look——' he began, making the familiar lightning change to seriousness. 'Ordinarily, I don't like anyone except senior cast and crew to see the rushes . . . it can backfire. But tomorrow I want you to come along and see for yourself what I'm up against, then maybe you'll be able to understand my point of view. As for Finn—well, I can accept his beefing and his malicious tongue, he's always been like that, but this is something else. He's having some problems at the moment, personal problems, and it might be wiser for you not to get involved.' He inspected his long fingers with a sudden, absorbed, interest. 'I suppose, though, if you really want to help him I could make you, rather than Mira, responsible for getting him on-set on time.'

'Oh, no thank you,' Joanna said with a swift firmness. 'Becky's enough of a responsibility.'

He sighed. 'If you say so.' His downcast eyes were screened by the thick, short lashes. When he lifted them, Joanna found herself looking into a baby-bland greenness. She frowned suspiciously, while he smiled innocently.

'OK, Joanna, if that's the way you want it, let's consider each other warned, mmm?' Her suspicion that she had just been manipulated was strengthened, but he distracted her by continuing, 'Now, we'd better front up outside, before everyone begins to think that we've murdered each other. But, before we do . . .'

Joanna blinked enquiringly as he picked up his stick and stepped closer towards the door. His mouth swooped on her upturned face, zeroing in on her lips before she had had a chance to decipher the devilish expression in his smiling eyes.

The caravan seemed to rock, and Joanna grabbed his shoulders steadyingly, her mouth parting in astonishment at the inquisitive thrust of his tongue. A hand was clenched in the small of her back, the head of the stick tapping her spine, another hand sliding softly under her jaw, thumb tugging her chin down as the warm muscle of his tongue stabbed and parried her inadequate defences to slide past and taste deeper delights. When she tried to protest, Joanna's tongue tangled with his, and produced a satisfied groan from the depths of his chest. The long, hard body supported her lighter one, the hand on her jaw sliding up under her hat to rake through the silver thatch of hair and pull her head against his shoulder.

Joanna couldn't believe her own passiveness, although she was not entirely passive, for her whole body was fraught with a weird and wonderful tension that begged to be satisfied with an even closer contact. She hung on his mouth, able, in the midst of the bewildering assault of sensation, to admit that he kissed better than any man she had ever known . . . his kiss, in fact, was as good as he looked . . . better, she decided, as her throat arched to the demand of his mouth, to the playful intensity of lips, teeth and tongue.

When he drew back, a breath away, she blinked at him, drifting slowly back to reality.

'That's funny,' he murmured, his lips touching hers with feather-light softness as they formed the words, 'I thought I'd remember if I kissed you. I might forget a face, or a name, but never a kiss.'

Joanna struggled out of his arms and he let her go reluctantly. She pulled her hat firmly over her ears. That kiss bore no resemblance whatsoever to the last one he had given her . . . no wonder it didn't ring any bells for him! Her ears, however, were ringing frantically and she was shivering hot. His face held a mixture of puzzlement and arousal and, when she saw the tongue that had lately tasted her stroke curiously over his sexy lower lip as if the taste still lingered, she went almost as pink as her hat.

'That skin of yours is like an emotional barometer,' he marvelled, stroking a finger across her flustered cheek, 'it's so incredibly thin.'

What a horrifying thought! Joanna gathered her tattered composure. 'Thin, but tough,' she warned him, her brown eyes brazening it out with his.

Richard, being Richard, rose magnificently to the silent challenge.

'Sure you are. Do you want to hang around in here for a few more minutes, Rambo, until you look less frantically kissed?'

Joanna saw red, and it wasn't his hair! Her hand shot out and landed a sharp, satisfying smack across that smart mouth.

'Do *you* want to hang around, Don Juan, until you look less deservedly slapped?' she asked sweetly, through gritted teeth.

'"These violent delights have violent ends",' Richard murmured, unoriginally, as he watched her fling out of the van, wry admiration warring with a desire to drag her back inside and really ruffle those female feathers. His little owl was proving to be a rare creature indeed, a woman who seemed to be wholly unimpressed by who he was. He couldn't intimidate her either ... if anything it was the other way around! Joanna Carson was a very unexpected woman.

He rubbed his stinging jaw thoughtfully, exploring the uniqueness of his feelings towards her with pleasurable surprise. He smiled slightly at his conclusion. He considered himself a conservationist, didn't he? In view of the delightful rarity of his snowy owl, it behoved him to take an active interest in her welfare. If he did nothing he might be contributing to the extinction of a species! Freckles hadn't looked Joanna's type at all—too stolid, too calm ... he'd want to cage her with practicalities. Richard didn't want that—he wanted to soar with his owl, protect her from predators, give that lovely temper of hers a healthy airing every now and then with a dose of his. Loving and fighting, his instincts told him that she'd do both well, and Richard always went with his instincts!

CHAPTER FOUR

'She's *awful*.' Joanna sat, stunned, in the semi-darkness of the hotel conference room which had been hired for the showing of rushes.

'I did warn you.' Richard Marlow signalled his thanks to the cameraman who had run the projector, and slid sideways in his chair to watch Joanna blink awkwardly as the room lights came on.

'I know, but I thought ...'

'That I was exaggerating . . . I do tend to cry wolf, don't I?' He shrugged ruefully.

'She's so wooden . . . surely you won't be able to use any of those scenes?'

'It's amazing what a little judicious cutting can do.' He seemed remarkably undismayed.

'I don't understand why you chose her in the first place, if she's so . . . so . . .'

'Awful?' He picked up the hand she had unconsciously clenched in her lap. 'We didn't have formal auditions, and the screen tests we did weren't scripted . . . it was her *personality* which attracted me.'

Joanna's eyes snapped wide and he sighed. '*Not* personally, Joanna . . . professionally. She's very outgoing, she has determination, she's eager to learn and she's not inhibited about expressing herself.'

'And that makes a good actress?'

'No, but it's a start. The most important thing of all was how she looked on the screen.'

Joanna had to admit that Becky had looked not merely lovely, but extraordinarily beautiful on-screen, but she was disappointed that such superficialities were more important to Richard than the quality of acting. She had thought, from the respect with which people spoke of *Foreign Tongues*, that he had rejected Hollywood trappings. She pulled her hand away from his, ostensibly to smooth out the wrinkles in her woollen skirt.

'Joanna . . .' His exasperation showed that he could read her mind with disconcerting ease. 'The greatest actor put on God's earth would be no use to me if he couldn't come across on film. Film has an almost human capacity to love and hate. There are some people who, no matter how much they try, can't look bad on film. You can dump them straight in front of the camera, cold, and they'll carry it off by their sheer screen presence. Becky is one of the lucky ones. All she needs is guidance and training to help her flesh out that potential. Did you notice that first take in the kitchen scene with Joe? It was great, wasn't it?—exactly what I was aiming for. But Becky didn't even realise that we were filming because I got Jeff to shoot the camera rehearsal. She was natural, relaxed, beautifully unaware. If I have to keep cheating a performance out of her like that, I'll do it, but I happen to think that she is capable of producing it herself. Once she realises that, there'll be no stopping her, I know it in my bones. Trust me, Joanna.'

Joanna stared at him warily. Oh, yes, she wanted to trust him. How could a man who kissed like he did be anything but trustworthy? She felt light-headed just remembering that kiss in the caravan. Thank the lord for her dignity that he hadn't followed up the advantage! He hadn't even mentioned it since, but he had a certain way of looking at her mouth that curled her toes.

'For God's sake!' he exploded, misinterpreting her silence. 'Everyone else in this damned company believes in me, why in the hell do I have to work so hard to convince *you?*'

'Everyone else is *not* Becky's chaperon,' Joanna said hastily, guilty that she had allowed her thoughts to stray so far into forbidden territory. But then Richard had that effect on her. Up until now Joanna had cheerfully accepted the opposite sex as different, but not disturbingly so, good companions rather than potential lovers. Richard only had to come within ten feet of her and all her feminine defences flashed out the warning: MAN.

He said a rude word and laid a hand over his heart. 'Joanna, I swear to you on my dear mother's grave that I have no nefarious designs on your niece. The aunt, now, she's a different matter . . .' His lazy smile sent a rush of quivers down her spine. She suddenly noticed that everyone else had left the conference room to go down to breakfast.

'Your mother isn't dead,' she said, quellingly.

'She will be by the time I've convinced you of my sincerity. I'll probably be decrepitly impotent myself. I admit that Becky is young and lovely and nubile and, quite probably, I could make her willing, but *I* am not. I was never wildly promiscuous anyway, not even in my Hollywood salad days.'

'That's not what the newspapers said,' she felt driven to say.

'So? Is the printed word automatically gospel?' He was definitely annoyed now. 'Believe me, the Hollywood press are a pack of wolves. I couldn't smile at a woman without them embroiling me in a passionate love affair with her. And if I *didn't* smile that automatically meant it was a *secret* passionate love affair. Sure, there were women——' His gaze was bold and direct. 'Considering the quality, quantity and availability it would have been something to write about if I hadn't taken up the occasional offer, but I'm not a stud carving notches on the bedpost. I'm a damned good director, Joanna, and I intend to prove it. I'm certainly not going to jeopardise my authority on the set by becoming intimately involved with a member of the cast. I will, however, give her all the support and encouragement that she badly needs and, in spite of what you obviously think, I can do that without having to take her to bed.' The smooth voice was becoming increasingly choppy. 'And I don't know why the hell I should have to explain this to you!'

Nor did Joanna. She felt ashamed of herself; especially since, in the middle of his tirade, she realised that it wasn't entirely for Becky's sake that she was throwing up doubts. It was partly to combat her own increasing attraction for the man now standing aggressively before her. She sought for a way to apologise without revealing her uncomfortable discovery.

'So what you're telling me is that your reputation as a director doesn't depend on your prowess in bed.'

'*What?*' The outrage was as swift and explosively genuine as she had expected.

'That's very clever,' she said, admiringly. 'Is that

something you learn in acting school—to howl between clenched teeth?'

Three very long seconds ticked by as he stood staring furiously down at her. Joanna stared back, feeling wickedly pleased with herself. He couldn't stay angry with her now without appearing unable to take a joke . . . and she guessed that Richard was rather proud of his warm sense of humour. She felt a tiny nip of delight as she watched the realisation take hold of him, the reluctant admiration enter the hard green eyes, although he still looked as though he would take pleasure in strangling her.

'I think *you're* the clever one,' he said slowly, at last, still unwilling to smile.

'It comes with the territory,' she told him smugly, and then, because she owed him, 'I'm sorry, Richard. Perhaps I have more of Ellen in me than I'd like. It's just that, for all her fine front, Becky is still very naïve . . . I would hate her to be hurt.'

He smiled then, at her gracious apology *after* she had salvaged her pride. 'Hurting her is the last thing I want to do. I'm not an insensitive clod, Joanna, nor am I totally inexperienced at dealing with girlish crushes. Women have thought themselves in love with me before, and survived the discovery that I have feet of clay.'

The self-mockery was cynical and yet disarming, and it laid every last, niggling fear to rest far more effectively than his earlier, reasoned argument. Joanna could go happily with her instinct on this one, and her instinct was to trust him.

The next few days proved her right, as Becky began to blossom before the cameras. Her performance was still uneven, but Richard cleverly used her uncertainties by focusing on scenes where Helen was discovering her own uncertain emotions.

Fortunately, as Joanna tried sturdily to convince herself, her own relationship with Richard wasn't allowed to blossom similarly, for Nick Fellows arrived to shatter the new ease between them.

He appeared on-set the day they were shooting interiors at a huge, old, rambling mansion on the outskirts of New Plymouth. Other than film equipment and the set-dressed kitchen, the house was empty; draughty, dusty and gloomy was the consensus.

'Darling! We can't go on meeting like this!' He greeted Joanna with typical theatricality, and helped himself to a plate from the trestle-table the caterers had provided in the high-vaulted, echoing dining-room. 'Stuffing your face, as usual, I see,' he had continued cheerfully, as if they were still student friends who had never lost touch.

'I see I don't have to introduce you two,' Mira had grinned, handing Jeff Hobbs a plate of pizza. There was no physical resemblance between them so, in spite of the identical surnames, Joanna hadn't realised that they were father and daughter until Suzy had told her. Mira had dreams of becoming a camerawoman herself, but on her own merits, not those of her father.

'I'm an old flame, aren't I, Jo?' Nick stretched the point with a grin.

'A *very* old flame. In fact, you might call him an ash,' she said drily, finding herself a stray equipment box to perch on while she ate.

'An ember, sweetheart, an ember!' Nick protested laughingly, plonking his jean-clad rear on the floor beside her. 'We were soul mates at University.'

'What were you studying?' Suzy Layton's blue eyes checked out Joanna, before they fixed on the new arrival with interest. Joanna shook her head, with a grin to indicate that Suzy was welcome, and the actress winked in reply.

'Economics.' Nick was returning the compliment, and liking what he saw. 'But I discovered that my heart really belonged to the theatre. I'm afraid I neglected my studies shamefully. It was only beastly swots like Joanna who could combine the two and come out tops in both.'

'You've done some acting?' Suzy's attention shifted back in surprise to Joanna, who shrugged awkwardly.

'Some?' Nick had no such reticence. 'She was our resident star. Had the lead in our outdoor Shakespeare production three years running.'

'Was she any good?' The drawled enquiry came from the doorway, and Joanna saw Richard saunter in to pick idly at the table. She couldn't interpret the look he gave her, but it wasn't the warm friendly one that she had become used to fending off.

'She was fantastic!' Nick had always been more enthusiastic about her acting than Joanna had been. 'There practically used to be fisticuffs to get to play opposite her, just for the reflected glory. I don't think she ever got a bad review.'

'Spare my blushes, Nick.' Joanna was exasperated. Her experiences were very small beer in this distinguished company. 'It was all strictly amateur stuff.'

'Don't be so modest, Jo.' Anyone would think Nick was being paid as her publicity agent! 'She could have turned professional straight away, if she'd wanted to,' he told his interested audience. 'Someone from The Circle saw her Beatrice, and invited her to audition for the company. She would have strolled it, but——'

'But I wanted my degree.' Joanna thought it time to stop him, knowing what he was going to tell them. Her ignominious fall from grace, both literally and figuratively, during rehearsals for *School For Scandal* belonged firmly in the past, no matter how entertaining a story it might make. 'I wanted to be a teacher, not an actress.'

She resigned herself to the looks of disbelief. It had been the same back then. People had seemed to think that talent was synonymous with ambition, and the peer pressure had been subtle but persistent. Joanna had been secretly relieved when her eyes had suddenly developed their irritating sensitivity to make-up and bright light. It had given her a legitimate excuse to 'retire' from the hobby that had begun to devour her study-time.

'Strange you never mentioned such an *interesting* past,' Richard said pleasantly, and a piece of cold chicken caught in Joanna's throat as she finally identified the look in Richard's eye. Wariness. Suspicion. Now what had she said to prompt that?

'I consider my present more interesting than my past,' she said, after coughing to dislodge the chicken. She realised that had been the wrong thing to say when the suspicion hardened.

'And your future? Are you regretting lost opportunities? Ready for new ones?' Joanna wondered if she was the only one to detect the sardonic thread.

She stiffened at his tone. Did he actually think that she was angling for a part in his film? That she had been playing some devious game to get his attention, in order to promote an acting career?

'No, of course not. I find teaching very satisfying,' she said, and then was annoyed with herself for dignifying his supicion with a defence.

'But surely you wouldn't turn one down if it came along or——' his eyes flickered to where Becky was carefully selecting a plate of non-fattening fare '——thrust itself upon you.'

'I would, actually.' She kept her voice cool and steady, though she longed to throw his veiled accusation back in his teeth. It reminded her forcibly of one of the reasons the theatre had not appealed to her as a way of life—the claustrophobic intensity with which the Great God Art was pursued. For all their talk of 'interpreting life', actors lived in a tight, enclosed world, circumscribed by the generally anti-social hours they worked.

Of course, he hadn't believed her. He hadn't said so, but it was obvious from the way he had distanced himself ever since ... no teasing banter, just a slightly sarcastic politeness. Joanna, who wasn't used to having her integrity called into question, responded with a stiffening of pride.

Let him think what he liked! She should welcome his abrupt lapse of interest. She had been only a temporary challenge to him, anyway. She didn't really have what it took to fix the interest of a man whose life was filled to the brim with colour and excitement, even supposing she had wanted to!

'Cut. Cut. *Cut!*' Joanna began to knit faster as Richard sprang up the steps of David's shack, his voice shimmering with repressed frustration. This was the first of Becky's really difficult scenes, and it was going badly. She was far too nervous, and her over-reactions were spoiling the finely balanced moment when David first reveals the desire he feels for the girl/woman who has insinuated herself into his solitary life.

Snapping out a command for everyone to stay put, Richard grabbed Becky by the hand and led her, on the verge of tears, across the uneven ground to the shelter of the generator van, sending a stray technician scuttling away on a manufactured mission with a single, expressive glare.

Joanna, muffled up in her favourite chair, was on the fringes of a bored group awaiting the call to their brief moments of intensive activity, but she had no trouble tuning out their idle conversations in favour of the important exchange going on several metres to her left. She could see both faces in profile, tears now glistening on Becky's cheeks; and the cold air carried every word to her with crystal clarity. Every *shocking* word.

'What would you do, Becky, if I told you that I was in love with you? That you've got me so tangled up with emotion that I don't feel able to direct you properly?'

'R ... Richard?' Becky was stunned, bewildered, her hand going out in appeal then dropping limply to her side. Joanna, frozen to her seat, felt a storm of anger, disappointment and sadness swirl around inside her. After all his fine words! Becky's hand came up again and Joanna half rose to rush to her rescue when:

'*There!*' The fierce roar of triumph made her almost drop her knitting. Everyone stopped pretending their indifference, and stared in earnest as Richard grabbed Becky's outstretched hand and waved it aloft. '*That's* the reaction I've been trying to get from you. What you just felt, what you just did with your hands and face. *That's* what I want from you!'

Joanna was shattered with fury as she realised that she had just been privileged to witness Richard in performance. He had wrenched apart Becky's emotions—and her own—for *effect*.

Richard, meanwhile, was blithely driving home the lesson with ruthless force. 'You were shocked by what I said, and what was your response? You didn't know what to do ... with your eyes, your hands, your words ... you didn't know what to say, or whether you were happy or frightened, so you tried to hide what you felt. That's what people do in real life, Becky, they don't project—they *protect*. So don't act when David makes his move ... try to show me nothing, but *feel*. Let the camera do the hard work, let us find you, not the other way around.'

He had reached Becky in a way that all his earlier, patient coaxing hadn't, even Joanna could see that. But she was still angry. She watched, faintly repelled, as Richard changed tactics and cupped Becky's face in his hands.

'Now I've been such an utter bastard to you, you can consider yourself well and truly baptised as an actress. But I wouldn't have put you through that if I didn't have faith in you, darling. Forgive me?'

It was a foregone conclusion. Becky floated away to get her make-up re-touched, face glowing with enthusiastic enlightenment.

'Had you going there for a minute, didn't I?'

'Not at all,' Joanna lied. So he had known she was within earshot. She gritted her teeth and refused to look up. 'You always ham it up when you know you have an audience.'

There was a small silence while Joanna tried to

concentrate on her knitting. She had never liked it, but it kept her hands occupied and scarves were supposed to be easy.

'It was for her own good. She needs to learn how to curb and use her emotions simultaneously, both good and bad. It all helps the toughening-up process, and she'll need to be tough if she's going to be an actress,' he said smoothly. Joanna snapped at the bait, looking up at last.

'Who says she's going to be an actress?'

The green eyes kindled and Joanna braced herself for a thrust. 'I would say that was up to Becky. Don't let your jealousy of her success stand in her way. I'm sure I could find a little part for her aunt to sweeten the sour grapes.' His eyes lowered and he smiled his satisfaction. 'Did you know you'd dropped an entire row?'

Joanna was still simmering when she sat down at dinner that night. A convention was booked into the hotel and the restaurant was full, so she was forced to take a seat at the long table—as far as possible from Richard. Finn, on her left, caught her curious look at the clear liquid in his glass.

'I wish I could say it was vodka, dear, but unfortunately His Lordship is in an uncertain mood so, for the sake of peace, I'm trying the local water,' he grimaced. 'I can feel my liver going into shock already.'

Joanna smiled as she started on her soup. She had learned that it was useless to query Finn's drinking. He even smuggled a flask into the rushes 'to relieve the tedium'. Joanna, braving Richard's cold shoulder, still attended, but sat beside Finn, trying not to giggle at his outrageous critiques of his own, and everyone else's, performances. That earned her even more sullen green looks.

Talking to Finn, and Suzy on her other side, when the young woman could drag her attention off Nick, meant that Joanna could avoid being drawn into the lively conversation at the other end of the table, but she was acutely aware of Richard's voice dominating the discussion. Would he let her get away with totally ignoring him?

'Our superstar giving you some professional tips, is he, Joanna?' She tensed when she heard the velvet voice aimed provocatively in her direction. 'A few hints about how to get yourself noticed? Take them with a grain of salt, won't you? A star's influence is pretty finite, whereas a director's . . .'

'We all know that's really why you switched to direction,' Finn drawled lazily. 'To satisfy the hidden despot in you.'

'The only influence I want him to exercise is over my school drama club,' Joanna said coolly, to show that Richard had not succeeded in getting under her skin. 'I thought Finn might give my kids a talk if he's got time before he leaves New Zealand.'

The dark red eyebrows crawled up mockingly. 'You teach drama? How interesting. What's the old proverb? "Those who can do, those who can't teach."'

A few glances went back and forth, as people registered the interesting undercurrents running the length of the table. 'At least teaching has a redeeming social value,' Joanna said tartly. 'We teach children to think for themselves, not just to mouth other people's words and ideas. But, if you want to argue this second hand, I can think of no better spokesman than Samuel Johnson: "Players, Sir! I look upon them as no better than creatures set upon tables and joint stools to make faces and produce laughter, like dancing dogs"!'

Varying displays of laughter and protest greeted this outrageous pronouncement.

'How pompous and self-righteous of old Sam,' Richard replied blandly. 'Fortunately, I escape his censure, since I'm no longer a mere *player*.'

More protests erupted, Becky's riding highest. 'But you're not really giving up acting completely are you, Richard? You can't! It would be such a waste. You have so much to give.'

'You're too kind.' His modest smile set Joanna's teeth on

edge. 'Fate has, apparently, decreed otherwise. I never wanted to devote myself entirely to screen acting, it's too easy to lose touch with the basics, and I'm afraid that stage work takes the kind of physical stamina that I don't have any more.' The sensuous mouth twisted with self-mockery. 'Not for lead roles, anyway, and I don't think that I could reconcile myself to spending the rest of my life doing walk-on character parts. My *ego*,' with a little bow in Joanna's direction, 'demands more than that. I'd rather give it up than starve on half a loaf.'

The momentary silence was almost reverent, and Joanna punctured it with a snort. Couldn't they see that he was milking the part for all it was worth? It was a shame, sure, but not a tragedy of Shakespearean proportions.

'I don't know,' she said, with a challenging lightness. 'There's always Richard III—"so lamely and unfashionable". Tailor-made for you. Not only do you have the limp, but you have his spectacular talent for manipulating people and situations to your own advantage.'

The table was ringed with frozen faces. Even Finn seemed taken aback by the maliciousness of her remark. But Joanna silently stood by her conviction that Richard Marlow enjoyed playing on his injury when it suited him. She stared down into his glittering eyes. The tension stretched as everyone waited for him to put her succinctly in her place and rebut the heresy. Joanna felt her stomach tighten with each long second.

Suddenly, the icy green eyes splintered and, to the company's shock, Richard began to laugh. Uneasy grins became baffled smiles as they watched him give in to an uninhibited amusement.

'You screech owl, I bet you peck out the eyes of fledglings, too,' he said, when he brought his laughter under control, but the accusation, and his expression, held a certain tender admiration. He ran his gaze around their startled audience and grinned, approving the way her shock tactic had grabbed their attention. 'Perhaps I shall do Richard some day. Perhaps I should hire you as my coach, Joanna. Are you always so brutal with self-pity?'

'Self-pity, no. Self-aggrandizement, yes,' Joanna said, surreptitiously wiping her palms on her skirt under the table. For a moment there she had been afraid that her stab in the dark had hit him in the heart. She hadn't wanted to really hurt him, just show him that she wasn't an easy target for his gibes.

'To that end, why don't we stop talking about me and talk about you?' Richard deftly turned the point of the conversation against her. 'Why don't you tell us why you gave up acting? Or did it give *you* up?'

'A bit of both, I guess,' said Joanna, uncomfortable in the spotlight. 'I enjoyed it, but acting was just one of a number of interests in my life at the time and, past a certain point, it wasn't worth continuing unless I wanted to concentrate on it to the exclusion of everything else.' Out of the corner of her eye she saw Nick lean forward to say something, and quickly added, 'At that stage, too, my problems with my contact lenses were getting worse.'

'Joanna has very sensitive eyes,' Becky informed everyone readily, snatching attention for herself. Joanna noticed that lately she had been dropping the 'aunt'—very adult. 'She can't wear make-up, even hypo-allergenic stuff, with her lenses in. And, well . . . you could hardly have a Juliet in glasses, could you?' She laughed at her own innocent joke. Or was it innocent?

'No more than a Hamlet with a limp,' murmured Richard.

Loren frowned thoughtfully from half-way down the table. 'You mightn't have the same problems in film as in theatre, Joanna. Your skin is flawlessly coloured. You could probably get away with almost nothing.'

'It's not only cosmetics, it's bright light as well,' Joanna said, feeling her eyes begin to prickle with a sinking of her heart. She had a Pavlovian response to any mention of her eyes, her tear ducts immediately anticipating trouble. Damn! She widened her eyes, but the feeling of discomfort increased.

'Besides, the matter is purely academic . . .' Fighting off a sudden stinging in her left eye, Joanna hardly heard Richard's heavy sarcasm, '. . . since Joanna is so adamant that she prefers social redemption as a public servant to nurturing and expressing talent as an individual. Having been thwarted at the latter, it's only natural that——' Joanna could stand it no longer, she jumped up.

'Excuse me,' she muttered, pushing away from the table and rushing blindly out of the restaurant, fumbling in her handbag for her eye-drops as she reached the foyer. She couldn't find them, and she swore feelingly.

'Joanna?' A hand caught her arm, swinging her around. 'Oh God, I didn't mean to make you cry——' Richard's voice was husky with remorse. 'Does it really mean so much to you? I *am* a brute. Joanna——'

'I'm not crying,' she said fiercely, pulling away to stumble over to the mirrored wall on one side of the foyer, nearly stepping into the ornamental pond in front of it in the process.

'Then what are those wet things sliding down your cheeks?' Richard's voice was gentle in her ear.

'It's one of my lenses . . . oh, damn it!' In desperation, she ducked her head and gave the corner of her eye a tiny tug, flicking out the lens into the palm of her hand. Relief was instant and delicious, but now she felt like a drunken sailor, one eye crisp and clear, the other a wild blur. She went to turn and halted, feeling hopelessly unbalanced.

'What's the matter?'

'Nothing. Go away——' His concern made her feel even more vulnerable, and she needed to be strong around Richard Marlow. 'Where's the Ladies'?' She resisted the urge to lean on Richard and ask him to guide her. A woman might find excitement, delight, passion, in his arms, but never safety. She turned back to the mirror and put the lens in her mouth.

'What are you doing?' Richard demanded immediately. He had an almost childish sense of curiosity, Joanna had discovered, and an equally childish brashness in asking questions. He would call it honesty.

'Lubricating it so that I can put it back in. It won't be as comfortable as using wetting solution, but I seem to have left that in my room. Now, would you mind going away?'

He was slightly behind her, watching, absorbed. 'Not until you apologise for what you said.'

'*I* apologise!' Joanna glared at his image in the mirrored wall, tucking the lens carefully in a snug corner of her mouth. 'You're the one who should apologise—for implying that I'm a scheming, thwarted actress. At least my remarks have the decency to be true. You *do* play on that limp. Your leg can't be that much of a handicap because I've seen you sprint on it.'

'Oh, when?'

'When I chased you across the——' She caught herself just in time.

'Cornfields? Bed?' His voice was beguilingly hopeful.

'Oh, shut up!'

'You started this little game,' he pointed out. She could hear, but not see properly, the grin. 'You were so frantically intriguing that you can't blame me for getting suspicious when a lovely little ulterior motive comes begging along. It's been done before. That woman at the film première, for instance, the one trying to impress me with her statistics . . . she was angling for a part. Some people will go to incredible lengths——'

'Not me!'

'Shame. Now, if *you* tried a strip-tease for me, I might react differently!'

Oh yes, he would react with a laugh. Anything more

unerotic than her angular slightness she couldn't imagine. Skinniness just wasn't sexy . . . stripped or clothed it was just the same . . . endless plains where there should be hills and valleys. Joanna wondered what it would be like to have flesh on her bones, to be desirable to a man like Richard, who had escorted some of the most beautiful women in the world. Imagine being undressed with reverent admiration, imagine being proud of your nakedness, your ability to arouse . . . Joanna's throat went dry and she swallowed hurriedly. A strange, pained expression crossed her face.

'Joanna . . .? Put that thing in and come back to the table. I promise I'll mind my "ps" and "qs".'

'I think I'd rather go up to my room,' she said, in a stifled voice.

'It's too early. Please, give me a chance to grovel properly. Besides,' he added, cunningly, 'I might be tempted to seduce Becky in the absence of your tempting self.'

Joana gave him a hunted look, not responding to his flirtatious humour. 'I want to go to my room,' she said stubbornly.

'For goodness' sake, you're not embarrassed about me watching you replace that lens, are you? I promise I won't find it disillusioning. Hell, I've worn the things myself—in *Cedar Hills*, to change my eye colour—so I know what a bitch the things can be. Go on, pop it in and then come and have some dessert. You've only had three courses, you must be starving!'

She glared at him with such ferocity that he was taken aback.

'Joanna?'

'I swallowed it,' she muttered.

'What?'

She repeated herself, more inaudibly still.

'You what?' She closed her left eye, to see his mouth drop open.

'I swallowed it. I swallowed it!' She was yelling at him now, because she could see the mirth building behind his face. Sure enough, he cracked and began to laugh, leaning against the rocky edge of the fountain pool so that she could see two laughing Richards, one real, one mirrored, to double her humiliation.

'It's your fault!' she exploded. 'You distracted me. I *told* you to go away!'

'Oh God, what do we do now? Rush you to hospital to have your stomach pumped? Or just wait until it emerges naturally?'

'Very funny, Richard Marlow,' she said hotly. 'I'm going to bill you for a replacement, you know. I hope it torpedoes your rotten budget!'

'What shall I do in the meantime? Get you an eye-patch and parrot from props?' He was enjoying himself wickedly.

'Richard—if you ever, *ever* tell anyone——' She imagined her embarrassment increased twenty or thirty-fold.

'I won't, I won't,' he gasped. 'But we'd better invent a story that everyone can swallow——'

That was the last straw. Infuriated, she kicked out and more by luck than by aim succeeded in kicking his stick from under him. He staggered, still shaking with laughter, and Joanna met the outraged stare of a passing matron whose face told her exactly what she thought of young women who attacked helpless cripples.

Blushing with anger and embarrassment, Joanna navigated herself, one-eyed, to the lift, abandoning her tormentor. Her last sight of him, just before the door closed, showed the matron fluttering about him, her mottled face flushed with excitement as she realised who it was that she was attempting to help. And Richard, curse him, was playing the martyr, acting with charming helplessness as he grinned over the woman's broad shoulder at Joanna's dishevelled retreat. She should have kicked him into the fountain!

CHAPTER FIVE

JOANNA took out her other lens and threw it into the bathroom basin. She turned the cold tap on full and watched, without the slightest compunction, as the tiny lens whizzed around the sides of the basin a couple of times before disappearing down the plug-hole. Goodbye for ever! From now on she was going to be comfortable, and vanity be damned.

She rummaged through the carry-all in the double wardrobe and emerged with a pair of severe, black-framed spectacles that suited her mood. Then she got into her striped pyjamas. She wasn't going back downstairs to provide Richard with further amusement. She grabbed the nearest book to hand and got into bed.

She didn't like Richard laughing at her vulnerability, it completely wiped out the satisfaction she had felt at the idea of him grovelling for her forgiveness for the way he had treated her recently. She glared at the voluptuous woman on the cover of her book. She didn't like him laughing at her, she didn't like him being sarcastic, she didn't like him being suspicious or guarded, and she certainly didn't like it when he tried to use that sweet charm on her. She didn't like him at all. The trouble with Richard was that he automatically flirted with every woman he met . . . why, he had even charmed that old bat in the foyer. Young, old, fat, thin, he still put on the act. How was a woman supposed to know what was real and what was acting?

'Not that I want to know,' Joanna told the pouting book firmly.

'Liar,' the glossy female silently scoffed, and Joanna

threw her on to the floor in self-disgust. Now who was putting on an act?

OK, so she'd be honest with herself. She *shouldn't* like him, but she did . . . and, sarcastic or not, any attention had been better than none at all.

She ticked off the reasons why she should thoroughly disapprove of him: he had an actor's full quota of fickle instability, he was exhaustingly volatile, he was spoiled by female adulation, and he had a regrettable tendency to treat important matters lightly. She sighed. All these things were more than offset by his attractive qualities . . . his physical appearance, his intelligence, his dedication to his craft, his great personal warmth and generosity and yes, even that wretched sense of humour.

But she was wise to fight the attraction. She had no real place in Richard's life, and he had no place in hers. A mild flirtation was what he had been offering, with, no doubt, the expectation of a brief fling in bed together. Perhaps if Joanna had been a progressive free-thinker she might have been tempted, but, although she was only twenty-three, her principles had been forged by an old-fashioned mother and sister. In her mind, love and commitment were a prerequisite to sex, though she had to admit that that particular principle of hers had never been severely put to the test. And it wasn't going to be now!

The bedside telephone rang and Joanna just prevented herself falling out of bed in her haste to answer.

'Joanna?'

'Oh, hello, Ellen,' she muttered weakly. Fool, who did you think it would be?

'You don't sound very pleased to hear from me.' Ellen had an unerring ability to detect a slight, and Joanna spent the next five minutes assuring her that of course she didn't mind her sister calling practically every night. Then there were more anxieties to dispel: Becky's schoolwork was fine, and no, Joanna wasn't letting her eat too many fried foods, or drink alcohol and yes, she knew cocaine was currently the fashionable Hollywood drug but she hadn't seen any signs of drug-taking among the cast or crew and no, no promiscuity either . . .

By the time she hung up the phone, Joanna was thoroughly out of patience and, as a result, was uncharacteristically snappish when Becky eventually came in.

'It's rather late, isn't it? What have you been doing?'

'I just have to use the bathroom,' Becky mumbled. When she re-emerged her face was well scrubbed, which could have accounted for the glow, if not for the nervous eyes and bee-stung lips.

'Actually, we were going over the bedroom scene,' she said to the reiterated question, while vigorously brushing her hair.

'Oh?' Joanna adjusted the spectacles that had slipped down her nose while she had dozed over her thriller.

'Yes, it's going terrifically well,' Becky gushed, her eyes not quite meeting Joanna's in the mirror. 'Richard makes it all seem so easy.'

'And Finn too, I hope,' Joanna murmured, thoughtfully.

'Actually, it was just Richard and me.' Becky continued hurriedly, 'Mira couldn't find Finn. Richard was *furious*. Do you think that Finn deliberately tries to upset him? I don't see why, after all, it was Finn who ran off with Richard's fiancée, not the other way around . . .'

Joanna knew a good red herring when she saw one. 'So how did you play the bedroom scene minus one of the major participants?'

'Actually——' Joanna had noticed how often Becky used that word when she was uncomfortable. 'Richard was really just going over motivations and techniques.' She took a breath and Joanna sensed a challenge. 'He did run through the kissing scene with me, though.'

Joanna raised her eyebrows. 'Lucky you,' she said mildly. It was the right response; Becky grinned.

'Mum would probably go spare.'

'One of the reasons I'm here and not Mum,' Joanna

grinned back. 'I think I trust you with Richard and vice versa. He might be a bit devious but I don't think he'd be underhanded——'

She stared as Becky grabbed her nightgown and disappeared into the bathroom again. Had that been a guilty blush? She frowned at the light under the bathroom door and then at the crumpled script that Becky had thrown on to the dressing table, noting the extra wadding of pink pages that denoted a re-write. A sudden disquiet came over her. She was standing by the dressing-table, flicking through the pink pages, when Becky came out in her sprigged nightgown.

'What's this?' Joanna managed to keep her voice steady, although inside she was beginning to seethe.

'Richard thinks the scene is more effective that way.' Becky tossed her head to indicate that settled the matter for her.

'You mean, nude?'

Becky flushed, though from anger or embarrassment Joanna wasn't sure. 'It's only a small scene, only a few minutes of the whole film. Most movies these days have nudity in them. I agree with Richard—it's . . . it's just *right* for the scene.'

'Of course you agree with Richard. When do you ever *not* agree with him?' Joanna's voice was now trembling with the effort of controlling her anger, which wasn't directed at Becky, but at Richard. It's true the scene wasn't totally explicit, but Joanna could just imagine Ellen's reaction to seeing her 'baby' bare all in full frontal cinemascope. No mother was that modern, let alone Ellen. And to think that Joanna had been lying in bed having treacherously warm thoughts about Richard Marlow, while all the time he had been perpetrating this . . . this outrage!

'Did Richard ask you not to mention this to me?' It was important to establish the facts.

Becky shrugged awkwardly. 'He said he wanted to talk to you about it himself . . .' She trailed off, watchfully warily as Joanna picked up the warm, thick red robe from the end of her bed, and thrust her arms into it.

'Oh, he's going to talk to me about it, all right,' Joanna said, grimly.

'He said you'd see that, in the context of the film——'

'Don't parrot Richard at me, Becky, I'm not in the mood for it,' Joanna tightened her belt with a controlled jerk, her eyes glittering with determination behind black-framed glass.

'It's only acting, Aunty Jo!' Beginning to show an anxiety that strengthened Joanna's resolve, Becky fell nervously back into the habits of a lifetime. 'Aunty Jo?'

'Nudity isn't acting, it's an intimate statement about one's self——'

'I'm not ashamed of my body!' cried Becky hotly.

'Of course you're not. It's how you use it, or abuse it, that makes the difference,' Joanna told her. 'A good director should be able to produce a scene that doesn't rely on old clichés or cheap thrills for its impact——' She had a lot more to say on the subject but she was addressing the wrong person. Barefooted, she strode towards the door.

'You're not going to see him *now*?' Becky breathed in horror, only just realising what her aunt intended to do. 'You can't, Aunty Jo. What will he think? He'll think I *asked* you to! I'll just *die*!'

'I'm not going to let him go peacefully to sleep while I worry all night about it,' Joanna said. She wasn't going to deny herself the satisfaction of venting her temper, either. First there had been Richard sniping at her, then that embarrassment in the foyer, and Ellen pursuing her over the telephone wires. This time she wasn't retreating.

'Please don't go, Aunty Jo.' Becky was almost frantic, rushing over to the door to try and stop her opening it. 'You can't—it's so *humiliating*! I'm seventeen, for goodness sake, I'm an adult, you can't treat me like this. If you do I'll never, never forgive you . . .!'

'You're not the one who's going to be humiliated, Becky,'

Joanna promised, as she wrested her niece's hand from the doorknob. 'Nor am I.'

'Aunty Jo, please,' Becky wailed after her. 'Oh—you're as bad as Mum. You're *worse* than Mum!'

The ultimate insult echoed in Joanna's ears as she rapped on Richard's door. It opened almost instantaneously, revealing Richard dressed only in low-slung denims.

'I had a hunch you'd come banging on my door. Come in,' he said, falling back as she virtually shouldered him aside, his eyes gleaming with faint amusement as he took in the aggressive spectacles, pyjamas and robe. 'Drink?'

'No . . . thank you,' she added belatedly. 'I——'

'Seat?' He sat on the plush velvet couch and waved her to the other end.

'No, thank you.' It was easier to be angry standing up.

'My head on a platter?'

'No!' She retorted, before she realised what he had said.

'That's a relief. You're looking awfully fierce,' he grinned.

'And you know why!'

He sighed, 'You saw the script. I wanted to explain first——'

'Oh, really? You mean, sometime *before* the première?'

'Becky's happy with the changes.' He ignored her heavy sarcasm as he stretched his arms and tucked his hands behind his head. The tight, compact muscles of his shoulders and chest rippled smoothly, the dark red hair under his arms and across his chest signalling his masculinity. The satiny, pale concavity of his stomach was landscaped by the thickening curls of hair that traced from the eye of his navel down to the perilously low band of the tight jeans. He had his legs spread, denim pulling tightly over the lean thighs, and Joanna was strongly reminded of the brash sexual arrogance of some of the young toughs in her class. But Richard was no adolescent, he knew very well the message that his apparently indolent arrangement of limbs was transmitting, and it had a definite purpose. He was trying to intimidate her with his maleness, trying to distract and disturb her. She ignored the blatant body language, and stared him dead in the eye.

'Becky has only just turned seventeen. She isn't mature enough to handle this kind of exposure or its long-term implications. Right now, all she cares about is pleasing you and I consider it utterly irresponsible that you should manipulate her hero-worship so selfishly. If you think I'm going to allow you to go ahead with this ... this ... *trash*——'

'*Trash?*' Richard vaulted to his feet, temper flaring as she hit him where he hurt—right in his artistic ego. '*Allow?*'

'Yes—*allow*. You may be the director on this film, but I'm effectively Becky's guardian, and we both know damned well that when her parents signed that film contract there was no nude scene in the script. So you can take your pretty charm and shove it! If you think that, after days of being treated as if I've got the plague, I'm going to allow you to worm your way around my objections——'

He began a slow clap which drowned out the rest of her angry words. 'Bravo, darling, you do rage magnificently. I begin to appreciate your friend Nick's wailing and gnashing of teeth about your loss to the stage ...'

'I don't *do* rage, Richard Marlow.' Joanna's eyes were molten brown as they nailed him to the spot. 'I don't *do* anything. I express my opinions, I interrelate with reality, not some fantastic world that I've conjured up for my amusement. *You're* the actor. You're the one who rehearses being spontaneous, who practises being sincere ... and then you're surprised when people don't trust you! The trouble is that you believe your own publicity, the great red-headed hero who always wins in the end. Well, you're not winning this one, chum!'

They stood, eyeball to eyeball for a few, long moments after she had finished speaking, then Richard tilted his head back and broke the tension.

His anger seemed to dissipate as quickly as it had arisen.

With a murmur of frustration he ran a hand through the bright hair she had just sneered at, and Joanna saw that it was damp. Shower or perspiration? He had just worked a long day, full of trauma and aggravating delays, and it hadn't finished yet. He showed no outward signs of fatigue but he must be mentally exhausted. And tomorrow would probably be no different. Even when the actual filming went well there were problems—equipment going astray, or breaking down, the weather causing delays, sightseers and fans making nuisances of themselves, backers arriving unannounced and expecting to be treated like stars themselves, and the inevitable chafing of so many artistic egos in close proximity to each other. No wonder he tried to smooth his path wherever he could by taking short cuts. The love scenes weren't scheduled until the following week . . . plenty of time for him to have approached Joanna. Her determination wavered.

'Look, Joanna,' he said, quietly gathering his strength. 'I truly believe that this scene needs more erotic impact. It's not going to be tacky or dirty, I'm not aiming to titillate. What I want to do is emphasise the naturalness of their coming together. This film isn't about the destruction of innocence, it's about the strength of love and how it can work as a purifying force. The passion has to be strongly felt because they're both strong personalities . . . only Helen hasn't realised the extent of her own strength and love at this point. But she does feel an intense sexual curiosity and attraction, and a trust in David as a human being as well as a man.' He spread his hands, elbows moving out, opening his torso to her in a gesture of vulnerability that invited her to trust *him*. Joanna caught the scent of male perspiration. Tired, then, and probably needing his sleep. Was a few hours a night enough for him? Joanna was suddenly aware of the weight of his responsibilities.

'You're talking about the film, Richard,' she said, her indignation slipping perilously away. 'I'm talking about Becky, not Helen.'

'All right, let's talk about Becky,' he said, seeming to sense the slight softening and following up his advantage. 'She has the makings of a promising actress and she has the guts to go after what she wants. She doesn't want to be patronised or babied, she wants to be the best that she's capable of being. Would you deny her that? She wants to do the scene this way because she can see that it will make her overall performance that much more convincing.'

'And was that her opinion before or after you kissed her?' Joanna didn't know what devil had put the words into her mouth but Richard, quiet, serious and humanly vulnerable, was seriously undermining her self-righteousness.

'Oh, for God's sake!' he erupted satisfactorily. 'What the hell are you accusing me of now? You're a drama teacher, you must realise that there's a technique to projecting a kiss on screen? Surely you didn't expect me to shove her into the scene cold and say "OK—kiss him". You're not that stupid! I *had* planned to have Finn take her through it but, as you know, he's never around when you need him. I thought he might have been off somewhere with you—he certainly disappeared very shortly after you did.' He stared at her suspiciously, the thought goading him to a further explosion that unfortunately flared completely out of Joanna's control.

'Well? So I kissed her a few times. It was all purely mechanical. I didn't throw her on the bed and ravish her, you know, it wasn't in the scene. What are you getting paranoid about a few kisses for? A kiss is only a damned kiss. You want proof?'

He snatched her against his bare chest and Joanna let out a breathy shriek.

'I'll give you proof!' he growled against her mouth, and then he was kissing her and it was exactly the same as last time. Joanna felt as if the world had dropped away from under her feet and she was dangling in space without a lifeline. His chest was hot against her stiffened hands, his mouth sheathing hers in warm, wet silk, his arms hard against her back, binding her to him. When he at last relinquished her mouth she parted her lips to suck in much-needed air, only to find that, along with the life-saving oxygen, she had inhaled the sweet quest of his tongue. It filled her mouth, caressing her taste-buds with his male flavour, the supple tip blindly seeking its pleasure.

Joanna's fingers flexed and curled over the curve of the strong shoulders as Richard moved his mouth in skilful enticement. It was lovely, a moment out of time, and his refusal to let her actively participate by trapping her tongue with the sensual demand of his own merely enhanced her sense of forbidden delight.

The kiss went on and on until, rebelling at her enforced passivity, Joanna closed her teeth against the stiffening thrust of his tongue and he jerked his head back.

Joanna felt the heat in her cheeks. She pulled back her hands from the temptation of his bare skin and nervously adjusted her glasses. Her hands were shaking, she noticed vaguely.

One corner of Richard's mouth curled slowly upwards as his arms reluctantly dropped to his sides. 'See? A kiss is only a kiss . . .'

Joanna was dumbfounded. *That* was *only* a kiss; a matter of mechanics?

'Forgive me for leaping on you like that, Joanna,' his voice was low, hinting at laughter, 'I'm afraid my baser feelings got the better of me.'

He was apologising? That was even more offensive. 'Yes, well, we'll just forget about it, shall we?' she said firmly, showing that she could take it casually, too. A kiss is only a kiss, she reminded herself severely.

'Good idea.' He was gravity itself, lids lowered to hide dancing eyes as he watched her studiously avoid looking at his face, or bare chest. That left the lower half of his anatomy, and she might get rather a shock if she fixed her attention there. She had enjoyed his kisses and now she was fluffing up her feathers trying to hide the fact. What a pity

she was wearing that thick robe, he would have liked to
know whether her body had responded as obviously as his
had, but she would probably slap his wrist for trying to find
out. He *had* learned one thing ... she was a sensualist.
Surely that, combined with her intelligence, would enable
her to understand what he was trying to do in his film? He
pulled up a chair and sat down, pointing to the couch to
display his good intentions, and crossing his legs in an
attempt to conceal and control his lustful ones.

'Please, Joanna, let's sit down and start all over again.
Perhaps you'll tell me what *you* suggest I should do with the
scene.'

'Allow Becky to keep some clothes on for a start,' said
Joanna, perching nervously on the edge of the couch, skin
still afire.

'While they make love?' Richard looked incredulous.

'We don't have to see them in the act,' she replied
stubbornly.

'You mean fade discreetly to crashing waves upon the
shore ... come on, Joanna, talk about unoriginal ...'

'And explicitness is so original?'

'If that's what's worrying you, we can always use a body
double ...'

'Everyone would still think it was Becky. She'd get the
fall-out.'

'Not if we gave it some publicity ... it might even be a
good angle to work ...' He half closed his eyes consideringly. 'But it would stuff up our schedule no end—we'd
have to find the right match.' Devilry gleamed. 'Of course,
we could always use you, you and Becky have very similar
colouring. Put some of that thwarted talent of yours to
work ...'

'I am not thwarted.' Joanna gritted her teeth. 'There are
people in existence, you know, who don't give a damn
about acting—even people who don't know, or care, what a
movie is—they're just struggling to survive reality.'

'But you're not one of those.'

'No—I'm one of your audience. You know, those people who come out and actually pay to watch you perform . . . without whom you'd be out of a job.'

'I take your point.' Very neatly, he conveyed his apology without having to voice it. About to ask him to do so, she noticed him staring at her bare feet. Probably thinking how big they were. She tucked them defensively under the drooping edge of her robe and he looked up to smile whimsically.

'A pity, though. I would have rather liked to have used you.'

'Don't be ridiculous. You know it couldn't have worked.'

'Why not?' His amused surprise was galling.

'Because,' she muttered sullenly.

'Because why?' He was going to make her say it, damn him.

'Because I'm nothing like Becky!' she snapped. 'She has a figure, I don't. I'm more likely as a body double for a *boy*. I wish you'd stop these juvenile attempts at embarrassing me.'

He laughed. 'You're embarrassed about your body?' He stopped, his eyes widening as she flushed miserably. Mr Universe . . . He pranced around quite happily half naked, even appeared completely nude in one of his films.

'That wasn't what I meant,' she mumbled, but her blush deepened and he didn't believe her.

'Joanna, you must know that you have a lovely body.'

She glared at him, unable to believe his insensitivity. She wasn't stupid. At school, it had been 'four-eyes' or 'sticks'. All the boys had liked her, but they had *dated* girls with breasts.

'You really think that, don't you?' he said, wonderingly. He shook his head and looked her over with delight. 'Joanna, don't you realise that you have a very attractive and distinctive gamine look. It's very sexy.'

'Sexy?' Joanna gawked at him. Richard Marlow,

Look what we've got for you:

5 FREE GIFTS

... A FREE compact manicure set
... plus a sampler set of 4 terrific Harlequin Presents® novels, specially selected by our editors.

... PLUS a surprise mystery gift that will delight you.

FREE MYSTERY GIFT

All this just for trying our Reader Service!

With your trial, you'll get SNEAK PREVIEWS to 8 new Harlequin Presents® novels a month—before they're available in stores—with 11% off retail on any books you keep (just $1.99 each)—and FREE home delivery besides.

Plus There's More!

You'll also get our newsletter, packed with news of your favorite authors and upcoming books—FREE! And as a valued reader, we'll be sending you additional free gifts from time to time—as a token of our appreciation.

THERE IS NO CATCH. You're not required to buy a single book, ever. You may cancel Reader Service privileges anytime, if you want. The free gifts are yours anyway. It's a super sweet deal if ever there was one. Try us and see!

Get 4 FREE full-length Harlequin Presents® novels.

Plus
this handy
compact
manicure
set

Plus
a surprise
free gift

▼ **PLUS LOTS MORE! MAIL THIS CARD TODAY** ▼

Harlequin's Best-Ever "Get Acquainted" Offer

Yes, I'll try the Harlequin Reader Service under the terms outlined on the opposite page. Send me 4 free Harlequin Presents® novels, a free compact manicure set and a free mystery gift.

108 CIH CAMY

PLACE STICKER
FOR 6 FREE GIFTS
HERE

NAME _____

ADDRESS _____ APT. _____

CITY _____

STATE _____ ZIP CODE _____

PRINTED IN U.S.A.

Don't forget...

...Return this card today to receive your 4 free books, free compact manicure set and free mystery gift.

...You will receive books before they're available in stores and at a discount off retail prices.

...No obligation. Keep only the books you want, cancel anytime.

If offer card is missing, write to: Harlequin Reader Service,
901 Fuhrmann Blvd., P.O. Box 1867, Buffalo, NY 14269-1867

superstar sex symbol, was calling *her* sexy? Not even the most flattering of her friends had ever called her that.

'Yes, you know—tempting, desirable, sexually stimulating. Slender and slim-hipped, long, long thighs and lovely high breasts . . .'

'I'm skinny and boyish.' Joanna's voice shrilled stubbornly over the fizzing in her ears, determined to deny what she was hearing.

'At the risk of being misunderstood, darling,' Richard cocked her a wicked smile, 'boyishness can be sexy, too. You have a beautifully subtle, supple body and the most gorgeous backside I've ever seen grace a pair of jeans . . . I wish you'd wear them more often than the baggy sweat-suit pants you parade around in.'

Sometime during that incredible speech he had managed to move from chair to couch without Joanna being aware of it. Now, with the brilliant emerald eyes looking deep into hers and the thick, honeyed voice working its seductive influence on her senses, she found herself wanting desperately to believe him.

'Is that why you looked at me like you did at that première, because you thought I looked so sexy?' she said with embattled breathlessness.

'I cannot tell a lie,' he murmured, placing his arm along the back of the couch and shifting confidingly closer. 'At the time I was amused by the contrast. But I'd far rather cuddle up to you than that piranha with the 38C cleavage.'

'How do you know it was 38C?' Joanna asked vaguely, trying not to look at his mouth, and only falling deeper into his eyes. They were so close she could see the flecks that flawed the emerald, a gleaming halo of them that ringed the hot dark centres.

'Because she'd already failed to do privately what she tried to do publicly,' he said with equal vagueness, wondering if she would let him touch her without taking flight.

'Oh!' Joanna's mouth formed a faint O that seemed to fascinate him. 'Why?'

'Why what?' Was he leaning even closer or was it an optical illusion produced by her swimming senses?

'Why did she fail?'

'Because the blatant bores me,' he whispered, only a murmur away. 'And besides, I prefer a woman I can fit in the palm of my hand ... like this ...' Their foreheads brushed as they both looked down at his hand, which had slipped inside the overlap of her robe and cupped her left breast. Joanna knew that she should push him away but she remained frozen, her heart thudding. 'See how sweetly you nestle there ...' His breath mingled with hers the instant before he kissed her, wine-warm and redolent with desire.

His kiss was soft and careful, a sweet, slow, gentle invitation so different from the last, fierce coming together that Joanna was quite undone. She closed her eyes and dreamily moved her mouth against his. So much for men not making passes at girls wearing glasses, she thought, with a delightful inward curl of laughter. They didn't even get in the way of Richard's delicate, languid exploration of her mouth. His hand tightened briefly on her breast before sliding away and her eyes flew open, mutely protesting. Stringing tiny kisses along the rosebud bow of her upper lip Richard hushed her as his fingers flicked at the large, flat buttons of her pyjama jacket. Then his hand was back, curving over the soft skin. He gave a soft groan as the tight peak scraped over the heart-line of his palm.

'Sweet and soft and downy ...' he swirled the words around her eager mouth, 'just how I thought you would feel. God, it feels good to stroke you ... does that feel good for you, little owl?'

Joanna gasped as his thumb dragged up the under surface of her breast to press lightly down on her nipple, release it and press again. It was like an electrical charge that lit up her whole body.

'Richard . . .'

'It does, doesn't it?' He wasn't listening, his mouth straying to find the warm, rapid pulse in her throat.

'Don't . . . Richard . . . we must be sensible,' she pleaded thickly, her hands against him but applying no pressure.

'Why?' The fiery red hair burnt her skin where it touched as his mouth moved further down, on past the ridge of her collarbone.

She couldn't remember herself as he pushed her back against the low arm of the couch, and she became aware of the rigidity of denim nudging the narrow curve of her hip. He wasn't just acting, he was aroused. Her body aroused him! The knowledge was an aphrodisiac, causing a hot surge of answering arousal. Her hands splayed out over the smooth, heated flesh of his back as she became prey to a whole series of utterly new sensations. Why had she never felt like this before? Why didn't Duncan make her feel like this when he touched her?

'You don't want to be sensible, not really,' he murmured, as he lifted his head to study the inviting mixture of passion and surprise in her face. His free hand traced the uncompromising black frames of her glasses.

'These tell me that you want to be sensible . . .' His hand fell heavily on to her breast-bone and then settled on her other breast, '. . . but these, these tell me what you *really* want. The body doesn't lie.' His fingers almost completely encircled her small breasts, drawing both their attention to the taut, dark centres. Joanna's shuddering, indrawn breath was controlled by the slight hardening of his grip as he arched his upper body away so that he could better see the evidence of her desire. His eyes were hidden by dark red lashes but, when Joanna dragged her eyes away from his hands, she went weak at the expression on his face, as stunningly erotic as his touch. The male beauty was intent, absorbed in sensual appreciation, utterly uninhibited in showing what he was feeling. With a soft murmur of pleasure he lowered himself slowly back down, closing his eyes completely as the hard muscles of his chest gradually crushed the small, ripe-swollen fruits in his hands, releasing an intoxicating rush of mutual pleasure.

'Oh God, Joanna, this isn't enough,' he groaned into her ear, his breath stirring the silky short strands of silver feathering her temple. 'I want to see you completely naked ... will you undress for me?'

'Why does it always have to be the woman?' Joanna protested huskily, faint with excitement at the idea but unable to conquer lingering self-consciousness.

'Because it's erotic.' He tempted her with tiny movements of his hands.

'It's just as erotic to watch a man undress for a woman,' she argued distractedly. She shouldn't be here like this but she didn't know where she was going to get the strength to deny the delicious invitation her body had accepted from his.

'What did you say?'

Startled by his sudden sharpness, Joanna stammered, 'I said ...'

But before she could repeat it he had pulled his stiffened body out of her arms and leapt to his feet. He paced rapidly back and forth, as Joanna blushingly buttoned her jacket with fumbling fingers.

'Of course, that's it—the perfect solution!' He stopped and swung around to confront her, his voice filled with an enthusiasm as intense as it had been a few moments ago in the midst of persuasive passion.

'What is?' she asked shakily, wondering nervously if he had something kinky in mind to stimulate his jaded tastes. Ought she to tell him how inexperienced she was?

'Finn can do the nude scene,' he flabbergasted her by saying. 'Becky needn't take off a stitch ... at least, nothing worth quibbling at. We can re-write the whole scene so that it doesn't take place in the cabin, but by the river.' He was pacing again while Joanna watched, unable to believe what she was hearing. 'Helen can come down to the river and see David stripping for a swim. But she doesn't go away, she stays and watches. She feels guilty, knows she's invading his privacy, but she can't help herself . . . she's excited, fascinated . . . and then he sees her. He's unashamed—bold—and she responds. She could walk into the water herself, fully dressed . . . God, yes, I can see it now . . .'

He certainly wasn't seeing Joanna as she stood up and tightened the sash of her robe, trying to ignore the throbbing in her breasts and the deeper ache that she only now acknowledged. She should be mortified at his bizarre rejection of a flesh-and-blood woman for a cinematic one, but her sense of humour rescued her pride. She doubted that even a Bo Derek would possess sufficient charms to recapture Richard's attention now.

'I must get this down . . .' Richard frantically searched for, and found, a pen amidst the chaos of the desk in the corner of the room. A clean sheet of paper was less easy to find and he looked around vaguely, his eye finally falling on Joanna, backing tentatively towards the door. He came towards her, frowning.

'Are you going?' The question was faintly harassed, as if he was aware that he should be showing some form of polite regret, but was for the moment unable to summon it. His mind was on greater things. Joanna took pity on him. Who was she to interrupt a genius at work?

'Yes, I think I'd better get back to Becky.'

'Don't tell her about this, will you?—not until I've hammered it out with Mal.' His frown suddenly vanished and he beamed at her and pounced, to give her an exuberant and totally passionless hug. 'Joanna, you're an inspiration. It's going to be a fabulous scene . . . I don't know why it didn't occur to me before to do it like this. I guess I'll see you tomorrow, hmm?'

He couldn't hide his eagerness for her to be gone, almost hustling her to the door, and she went obediently, ruefully admiring his lightning ability to alter the object, but not the intensity, of his absorption so completely.

He was on the telephone before she even closed the door.

'Mal? What? No, I don't, but it doesn't matter, you can sleep tomorrow. Tonight we have work to do. The love scene, I want to change it. I've got this great idea and I need you——'

And I need my head examined, Joanna thought wryly, as she retraced her steps down the hallway, letting him get away with treating me in such a cavalier fashion. Not to mention taking the credit for what had really been her idea! But how could she berate him, when she knew she should be grateful? If it hadn't been for his obsession with work they might have been making love right now, and tomorrow she would have despised herself for behaving like a sex-starved groupie. How would she have looked Becky in the eye? Or Ellen? Or Duncan?

Joanna paused before the door to her room and shuddered. How was she going to look *Richard* in the eye? What if he expected to pick up where they left off? She no longer had the security of imagining herself immune to his seductive charm, she had proved herself miserably susceptible—and he knew it, damn him!

She grinned suddenly. She did have one ace up her sleeve. She didn't *have* to rely on her own ability to say no, she could rely on his! All she had to do, if she found herself weakening again, was to throw out an idea for his beloved film, and he would be off and running. She giggled, her confidence returning—she could be out of control and still in control. The thought was extraordinarily satisfying.

But, as she tossed and turned in bed that night, one question nagged at her . . . Why, if she was supposed to be so grateful to Richard for terminating that traumatic bout of loveless passion, couldn't she summon up the least modicum of sincere gratitude?

CHAPTER SIX

To HER embarrassment, Joanna was wrong about Richard, he didn't hog the credit for the new love scene. In fact, he went out of his way to tell everyone that it had been all Joanna's idea, and then sat back and enjoyed the barrage of teasing that she had to endure. Finn in particular was merciless.

'You didn't have to go to all that trouble, Joanna,' he told her slyly. 'All you had to do was come and knock on my door and I would have been happy to strip off for you. Of course, turn about is fair play . . .'

At least her blushes seemed to slightly mollify her niece, who still hadn't decided whether to forgive her interference or not. She joined in the teasing, too, with a little too much enthusiasm sometimes, Joanna thought.

'Hey, Joanna, would you mind standing in for Becky for a few moments? She's still in make-up, and we want to check some lighting changes.' Dean's voice rescued her from yet another session of good-natured ribbing and Joanna agreed willingly, knowing that Becky's usual stand-in was off that morning, doing a small walk-on part with the second unit. It was part of the small crew's philosophy that nobody quibble at pitching in in an emergency, and Joanna was no exception to the rule.

'Stand here, will you?' Dean steered her past the equipment boxes that cluttered the entrance to David's cabin, and pointed to a mark chalked on the floor by the cast-iron cooker. 'How's that, Jeff?'

The director of photography consulted with his camera-man. 'On your toes, please, Joanna, Becky's a bit taller than you. Thanks. Hit the lights, Rex,' he called to the grip, and Joanna blinked as the blaze hurt her eyes.

'See what I mean?' Richard emerged from the dazzle to stand beside her. 'Too diffuse. I want it cool and harsh, but directional from the door, so we get lots of contrast shadow in the corners.'

'Yeah, OK, but we're getting bounce off her glasses, can we have them off?'

Joanna raised her hands to clutch protectively at her frames but they were gone, whisked away into Richard's breast-pocket. He compounded the crime by suddenly dissolving into the blurry mists of myopia.

'Turn your face to the redhead, Joanna.' She squinted wildly around to Jeff's instruction and settled on a vague red blob encompassed in a corona of light.

'Not *me*, dear girl,' Richard's drawl was punctuated by snickers from the crew, 'the light, the *light* . . . to your right. The ones with red tops are redheads, the ones with yellow, blonds. Haven't you picked up the lingo, yet?'

She couldn't dispute her ignorance without revealing her helplessness, so she suffered the taunt in haughty silence.

'More shutter on the blond, Rex, and angle the redhead a bit more,' Jeff peered through the lens himself. 'Now, walk over to the table, Joanna.'

'Come on, Joanna, we're not asking you to *act*.' The amusement vanished from Richard's voice as she desperately tried to remember the layout of the cabin. 'There's no Oscar yet for stand-ins, you know.'

The sarcasm propelled her into reckless action. After the crash, there was silence for a brief instant.

'I didn't mean for you to walk in a straight line. I did expect you to go *around* the stools,' Richard said, witheringly.

Hot and bothered and cross, Joanna snapped, truthfully, 'Well, I couldn't help it, I was looking at the table.' What she had thought was the table, anyway.

'It was right under your damned nose——!' he began to snap, when suddenly his voice switched to slow silkiness. 'Joanna—just how short-sighted are you?'

She glared vaguely in the direction of his voice, and nearly jumped out of her skin when his breath came warm in her ear from behind. 'My darling owl, you're as blind as a bat!'

She whirled to confront his blurry face. 'The light was in my eyes.' She widened the eyes in question, in a vain attempt to focus on his scepticism. 'Now, may I please have my glasses back?' She requested as sternly as her exposed vulnerability allowed.

'I rather like you without them,' he teased her, 'all fluffy and wide-eyed, a flustered bundle of helpless femininity.'

His breath came against her lips and she jerked her head to one side. 'I'm not *that* blind, Richard, stop it!' Fluffy, helpless? She was outraged.

'You're annoyed about the other night,' he murmured. 'I don't blame you, but I intend to more than make it up to you.' Precisely what she was afraid of! She stirred restlessly under his hands. 'It's just that you're proving to be such a sweet inspiration . . . in every way . . .'

'Richard, would you mind speaking up and giving us a voice level?' Garry Barrett interrupted the seductive recital before it had a chance to take effect, but Joanna's sigh of relief came too soon.

'Sure.' Richard raised his voice and poured forth its golden promise while his eyes caressed her pinkened face. '"She whom I love is hard to catch and conquer. Hard, but O the glory of the winning were she won"!'

Whom I love? Joanna gave him a brief look of haughty scorn, which he met with a whimsical shrug.

'Great, thanks, Richard.' Garry hadn't heard the content of the line over his headphones, only registered the bounce of the needle on his machine, and Richard's grin invited her to share the joke.

'OK, Joanna, we've finished now.'

She turned and gave a sweet smile in the general direction of the camera, plucked her spectacles from Richard's pocket, put them on, and stalked away without giving him another glance. His laughter followed her, as if he knew that her knees felt as weak as water.

Since filming had begun before dawn, and further night scenes were scheduled for after sunset, the afternoon was proclaimed a welcome break. Becky had already made her plans: with all her schoolwork up-to-date, she was going shopping with one of her old schoolfriends who had moved with her family to New Plymouth. Never one to particularly enjoy poking around in shops unless she had a purchase in mind, Joanna was happy to see the two girls go. It would do Becky good to indulge in some girl-chatter with someone her own age. The problem of what to do with her own afternoon was solved when Mira called to ask her if she wanted to take a trip up to the Manganui Ski Field to have a look at the snow. Joanna was an eager taker and, a few minutes later, was down in the hotel forecourt looking for the distinctive green station wagon.

Instead a large, dark blue Mercedes drew up and Richard slid out from behind the wheel to open the passenger door.

'All set?'

'Mira didn't mention that you were going,' Joanna said, reluctantly allowing him to urge her into the front seat.

'Didn't she? Naughty girl ... I wonder why not?' he grinned at her as he got back behind the wheel.

'Probably because she knew I wouldn't come. Hey! Aren't you going to wait for her?' As the car powered away.

'Why? Did she say she was coming, too?'

'Yes, she ... well, no, I just assumed ...' She frowned as Richard began to whistle. 'You planned this!'

'To the last detail,' he admitted smugly. When her frown deepened behind tortoiseshell frames, he coaxed, 'Come on, you wanted to see Egmont and the weather is perfect. Don't sulk and spoil it.'

'I do not sulk,' she said stiffly, thinking that this was the second time today that she had been manoeuvred into his company. He really did need to learn that he couldn't carry his direction over into other people's private lives!

'Do you like my car?' He cut across her brooding thoughts. 'I got one of the second unit to drive it down from Auckland.'

'This is yours?' Joanna looked in astonishment at the solid comfort of the interior. 'Somehow I thought you'd drive something more ... racy. This is like a tank.'

'I was cured of my taste for flash and dash in the States ... those things crumple like tin cans. Tanks are safer.'

'Do you ... do you remember much about the accident?' Joanna asked quietly, suddenly terrifyingly aware of how close he must have come to death.

'Not about immediately beforehand ... I only know that some idiot went through a red light into me. He was killed, so thank God it wasn't my fault; I would have had trouble living with myself. I can remember waking up though, in the dark, and smelling petrol and hot metal. It was wet, too, but when the cops brought in the lights I saw that it wasn't rain after all ... it was my blood—everywhere. Dark blood and glittering chips of glass and twisted metal, all rather horrifyingly artistic in a way. They had to cut me out ... the longest and loneliest half-hour of my life.'

'Richard——' There was no doubting the pain-hollowed sincerity of the graphic words. And she had mocked him about his injury!

He glanced at her briefly, and smiled at her compassionate horror. 'Don't go soft on me, Joanna. You hit the nail on the head when you hinted that I used the experience; I did. Fox would never have released me from my contract if I hadn't stretched out the convalescence ... I was too profitable in front of the cameras. They weren't about to allow me to waste any of my valuable time experimenting as a director. As it was, they let me go very cheaply and *voilà*, a director was born!'

'Do you miss it ... acting?' she asked hesitantly, but he answered easily.

'According to you, I'm still going strong . . . sorry, force of habit.' As she pulled a face at his flippancy. 'Yes and no. Acting always came naturally, directing is something that I have to work at. It's more of a challenge . . . uses all of me whereas, when I was acting, I only needed to use selected bits. Sometimes, when I run slap bang into the responsibilities, I wonder what the hell I'm doing it for, though.'

'That's how I feel about teaching,' Joanna said slowly. 'It's funny, the kids in my class are so tough and street-wise that people tend to take them at face value but, honestly, sometimes they're so naïve it sends chills up my spine to think of how unprepared they are for life. A lot of them are already locked into aggression as a way of hiding their ignorance or inadequacies, and that's a shame because they can be so damned nice when you show an interest, a real interest, in their point of view.'

'When you say aggression, do you mean in the classroom?' Richard frowned sideways at her slight figure. 'What does your headmaster friend have to say about that?'

Joanna resented the suggestion that she needed to hide behind a man. 'It doesn't usually get that far. I've been physically threatened a few times but, usually, it's just part of the act. I'm not big enough to be a challenge, you see, so they generally just content themselves with trying to say things that'll shock me into kicking them out.'

'Does that happen often?'

'I'm *almost* unshockable by now,' she admitted with satisfaction. 'I usually content myself with correcting their grammar . . . that tends to shock *them*.'

Richard chuckled. 'I'd love to sit in on one of your classes. You're like no teacher I ever had. I was a rotten scholar, too busy entertaining my fellows to take any competition from my teachers.'

'What do you mean, competition?' Joanna asked curiously.

'Well, in a sense teachers are actors, too, don't you think? Standing up there in front of the class, presenting your material in a way designed to catch your audience's interest. The only difference is that, unlike a theatre audience, yours can't walk out on you if you don't come up to scratch.'

'Oh, can't they?' said Joanna with a quirk, and proceeded to enlighten him as to the many and varied ways that her students showed their bored displeasure when confronted with some particularly mind-numbing subjects in the compulsory syllabus. His interest and amusement fed her own, and soon she was enjoying herself hugely, vying with him to see who could produce the most outrageous tale about their respective careers. From there, the conversation seemed to flow naturally to the subject of personal ambition—Joanna's not to be side-tracked, through promotion, into administration; and Richard's finally to shake off comparisons with his father.

'He casts a long shadow,' he said wryly, as he donned a pair of sun-glasses. They were heading directly towards Egmont now, and the sun, high in an arching sky, was bouncing brilliantly off the snowy slopes. 'I guess all of us in the family compete in our own way against our parents . . . but with Dad and I it's special, like Rosalind and Mum, since we're in the same field.'

'Was it an advantage, or disadvantage?' Joanna asked, expecting him to say 'both' with that flippant grin.

'Oh, definitely an advantage. The competition is immensely healthy, and Mum and Dad have never been condescending about my mistakes—and there were many in the early days—or offered the kind of gratuitous advice that my ego would have obliged me to reject. The atmosphere at home was always one of encouragement, whatever we wanted to do, and our opinions were always respected. My mother tells me now that they were a little concerned that Hollywood might go to my head, but all they said at the time was that I should take care not to lose my perspective.'

'And did it go to your head?' Joanna wanted to know.

'Like vintage champagne,' he grinned, 'for a while . . . it's a very alluring life-style. But a diet of champagne can be just as boring as a diet of bread, if you don't leaven it with something else. The accident happened just at a time when I was beginning to get indigestion . . . so I grabbed the opportunity to leave the table and ran . . . or rather, limped. When I told Dad I was going to try my hand at directing, he said that he wondered whether I had the strength of character, since I wasn't noted for my tolerance of other people's stupidity, and directing was "a constant struggle against the self-obsessed stupidity of actors".' He grinned reminiscently. 'The fur flew around the family dinner table that night! My father plays a mean devil's advocate, and my mother loves to play up to him. Since then, he's taken great delight in my success so far and even greater delight in telling me that, of course, I chose the soft option. Stage directing is the true art, a film director is merely a mechanic, he claims—thereby managing to draw my youngest brother, Charley, into the argument, too. Charley's a mechanic and, as far as he's concerned, it's the peak of achievement—to stick a *merely* label on it is sacrilegious.'

He went on to talk about the other non-artistic member of the family, his elder brother, Hugh, a commercial lawyer, and about his twin, Steve, who several years ago had split with his phenomenally successful rock band, Hard Times, to embark on an even more successful solo career. He talked about his sister, Rosalind, who was currently taking the female lead in a BBC costume drama, and *her* twin, Olivia, who was working on a portrait commission in New York. He made them sound like real people, warm and likeable, not just famous names that Joanna had read about in the newspaper and not really believed in. He also made them sound close, in spite of the miles between them.

'We are, I suppose,' Richard mused, when she said as much. 'We have our problems, like any other family, but we've always been brought up to respect each other . . . it makes the liking and loving so much easier. How about you? Are there any others between you and Ellen?'

'Sometimes I wish there were,' Joanna sighed. 'I was an accidental afterthought, you see—rather like Sam is. I was so glad when Ellen got married, because I thought it might take the heat off me. She's always been so infernally *organising*, and I was the most convenient person around to practise on. I thought that once she had a home of her own she'd want to fill it with little people to boss around but, funnily enough, she's not really instinctively maternal. Children are too disorganised for her to completely enjoy, and she always finds something extra to worry about, as if children didn't provide enough natural worries just by existing.'

'Mmmm, I know the type you mean. You, on the other hand, will make an excellent mother.'

'Yes, I will.' She was sure she was mistaken about that faint note of satisfaction, so she took the remark at face value. 'Because I'll make an effort to understand them, to let them breathe. I won't expect my children to be little replicas of me, but people in their own right.' She sighed. 'Ellen doesn't even approve of my teaching a special class. She thinks I ought to be at some toffee-nosed private school, teaching rich little darlings how to be fine ladies, not hooligans how to be the best it's possible for them to be.'

'It would bore you to death in a week.' Richard flatly confirmed her own opinion, as he attacked the winding road, edged with bush, that led up the lower slopes of the mountain. 'We're kindred spirits, you and I, we both respond to a challenge.'

Joanna burst out laughing. 'Alike? How can you say that, Richard? We're as different as . . . as . . .'

'As man and woman?' he queried, with a soft emphasis that jolted her back into the realisation that his motives for taking her on this outing were probably not the purest. Did he plan to lull her into a false sense of security, then pounce? Charm her back into his arms?

'Why did you tell me all that personal stuff—about your family?' she asked, suddenly suspicious.

'I wanted you to know,' he said, with aggravating simplicity.

'Why?' she asked, reluctantly, feeling they were approaching dangerous waters, but curious all the same.

'Because you seem to have some pretty odd ideas about me—most of them apparently culled from newspapers, or gossip, or hearsay, or roles that I've played. The public me is *not* the private me. I want . . . I need you to see me as I really am—a basically nice guy from a basically nice family. The kind of guy you'd like to have around.'

'Why is that so important? We hardly know each other, after all,' Joanna said, unnerved by the sudden seriousness of the rich, tonal voice.

The car drew up in a wide gravelled parking area surrounded by scrub, on what seemed to be a natural plateau. The car-park was nearly full. People carrying skis, or toboggans, or just dressed warmly against the cold, were passing through a gate at the upper end of the car-park, heading on foot up the mountain track, but Joanna was only aware of Richard unclipping his seat-belt and turning towards her, green eyes masked behind the sun-glasses, but the straight line of his mouth hinting at their intensity.

'It's important because I think I'm in serious danger of falling in love with you, Joanna Carson, and I want to be loved in return for myself not for some false image. I want you to learn to know me.' He traced her astounded lips with a graceful finger. 'You look surprised. Is it really so incredible? You're like no other woman I've ever met, Joanna, and that uniqueness intrigues and excites me.'

Joanna struggled to control her breathing, disgusted to feel herself melt inside at the huskily persuasive words.

'So that's why you keep such late hours, you sit up all night writing your script for the next day. You need a re-write man, Richard, your dialogue is atrocious.'

For an instant, temper tugged the corners of his mouth

and flared the aquiline nostrils, banishing the whimsical lover; and Joanna tilted her chin for the blow. Instead, he swore, and gave a short, exasperated laugh. 'And I thought that you weren't at all like your sister. You're a very stubborn, determined woman—fragile but strong. I like strength in a woman.'

'You like women, period.'

'I like people,' he reproved, his humour returning at her sniff. 'Some better than others. Come on, Joanna, we've got a fifteen-minute walk from here.'

Getting out of the car she shivered, not sure whether it was the cold or the delicious fear that Richard wasn't going to give up his erratic, inexplicable pursuit so easily. She pulled on her hat and wound her horrid, lumpy-but-warm scarf around her neck and set off beside him. For once, he was wearing a hat, dark blue like hers but infinitely more dashing, with the legend 'Aspen' knitted into the pattern.

His stride was naturally long, and Joanna found her thigh muscles protesting as she tried to keep pace, but her pride wouldn't allow her to ask him to slow down. The air was crisp and cold in her lungs, her breath coming out in frosty clouds, miniatures of those which drifted across the mountain, clearing every now and then to show the awesome peak. At first she was disappointed at the lack of snow on the stony track but, as they got further up the narrowing path, white patches appeared more often in the thinning scrub each side of them until, at last, they were filing up a mushy, slippery incline that had Joanna clutching at the wire rope which fenced off the sudden drop to their right. Half-way up there was an equipment lift on to which skiers loaded their skis and bags before plodding on up the path. Richard in his dark glasses, hat pulled down over the betraying hair, and scruffy sheepskin-lined suede jacket over well-worn navy-blue sweater and dark trousers, drew not a second glance from the groups of people they exchanged polite greetings with as they passed. It was like accompanying Clark Kent and knowing about his secret identity, thought Joanna with an inward grin.

When at last they reached the gently sloping area where
the ski-huts were located, Joanna looked around her with
delight. Children abounded, skiing and tobogganing, or
just sliding down the inclines on plastic sheets or scraps of
cardboard, or bombarding each other with snow. Outside
the ski-club, equipment was displayed for hire, while
further up the slope a ski-tow was taking those already
equipped up to a further level where a chair-lift operated.
Joanna could see numerous small, bright figures high up
what seemed to her like an almost vertical white wall,
zigzagging their way down, while higher still the rock and
ice summit lorded it over puny man.

'Can we ski?' She turned eagerly to Richard, having seen
the familiar logo on the wall of the ski-club. 'I've brought
my credit card.' She unzipped the pocket of her parka and
flourished it triumphantly. 'We can hire everything.'

'Do you want to?' Richard replied in a discouraging
voice, but Joanna was too fired by enthusiasm to take any
notice of his diffidence, or the slight tension that stiffened
his body. 'Have you ski'd much?'

'I haven't been to Aspen.' She slanted a tart look at his
hat, quick to respond to imagined criticism. 'But I've
certainly been on skis before.'

'I thought we'd just come up for a look——' he began, to
be cut off smartly. Was he afraid she'd make a fool of him?
She'd show him!

'I want to ski,' she said belligerently.

He sighed. 'All right, but I'm afraid you'll have to go up
on your own. Much as I'd love to join you, skiing is one of
the things I can't do any more.' He tapped his leg with his
stick.

'Oh, Richard!' Joanna covered her horrified mouth with
her gloved hand. 'I'm sorry, I forgot, of course I won't ski if
you can't.' Her eyes were mournfully big at her own
thoughtlessness.

His tension evaporated as quickly as it had come. 'You

can ski your heart out, silly owl,' he said softly, removing her hand to replace it with a gentle kiss. 'I'm delighted that you don't think of me as being handicapped. There isn't much I can't do, but anything that involves sudden, wrenching turns is included. Come on, let's kit you out.' He tugged her towards the skis.

'Oh no, I don't want——'

'Nonsense. I'd love to watch you flying down the slopes.'

Joanna blanched at his back. Perhaps she had misled him about her ability. But, having decided to be magnanimous, Richard would hear no objections. He even insisted on paying for the skis and putting them on for her.

'There!' He stood back and smiled. 'Now spread your snowy wings for me. I'll go up and get a coffee and watch you come down.'

'I thought I'd stick around down here, it's been a while since I ski'd,' Joanna said, nervously.

'Don't worry, it's like riding a bike. Have fun—go on.'

To her horror, he gave her a little nudge, and suddenly her feet began to slide away beneath her. She stuck one pole into the snow to stop herself but it only made her slew around, skis parting dangerously in different directions.

'Richard!' she wailed, as she discovered that the snow that looked so fluffy and soft was cold and hard.

Richard recovered from his astonishment to offer her a hand as she squirmed impotently around in the snow, entangling her skis in her poles.

'Joanna——' At the quiver in his voice she glared up at him. His face was entirely solicitous. 'Are you all right?'

'Yes, of course I am.' She ignored his hand, and eventually managed to get upright under her own steam.

'Joanna——' how well she knew that drawn-out lilt '——how long is it since you've ski'd?'

'A while.' She avoided his eyes by shaking out the snow from her parka.

'How long?'

She sniffed.

'Joanna—have you ever been in snow before?'

'Of course I have,' she said loftily, her delicate face tilted proudly at him.

'When?' he demanded, hands on hips, mouth twitching.

'When I was ten.' She fixed him with her most steely of stares.

To his credit, not a muscle moved in his face. 'My, that is a long time,' he said blandly, his voice slightly muffled. 'I don't think we'd better aim for the higher slopes today . . . if indeed this decade,' he muttered under his breath.

'What did you say?' Joanna dared him, sharply.

'I said, why don't we get a toboggan instead and *both* have fun? I mean, skiing does take an awful lot of energy and Becky did, well, mention that you . . . er . . . that you're not terribly co-ordinated when it comes to sport, that's why I didn't expect that you'd want to ski . . .'

'I can ski just as well as the next person,' Joanna insisted furiously. Unfortunately, the next person at that moment was a man who passed her in a snowy cartwheel, almost knocking her over again. When Richard had stopped laughing he sighed at the expression on her face.

'Stubborn wench. Come on. I'll teach you . . . over on the nursery slope though, where we're not going to endanger anyone's snowman.'

He was infuriatingly patient, in between hastily smothered fits of coughing that made her only more determined, especially since all around her children who looked as if they were barely old enough to walk were whizzing past her with total confidence. At last she coasted down a little slope without falling over until she reached the bottom, and Richard's glee almost matched her own.

'I think that's it for today, though, Joanna,' he told her firmly as she manoeuvred to her feet again. 'We can come back another time, but I don't think we're going to get any more sun today,' he pointed out, indicating the lowering cloud that now hid the upper half of Egmont, 'and you're pretty damp.'

She felt hot and sweaty, but was wise enough to take his advice, and bid a wistful farewell to the snow as they made their way back down the path. This time nobody passed them going in the opposite direction.

'I guess I got a bit carried away,' Joanna confessed over her shoulder as she negotiated the slushy track. 'It must have been boring for you.'

'I enjoyed every moment of it,' he said truthfully. 'If determination alone made champion skiers, Joanna, you'd be a medal-winner for certain.'

'Thanks for helping me,' she said. 'I suppose you were a brilliant skier.' She imagined him slicing a path through the snow with dramatic flourish, cutting a swathe through the ski bunnies, too.

'I was only ever average,' he confessed wryly. 'My flair was for après-ski, not sur-ski.' When Joanna looked around at him with a surprised giggle she almost slipped, and he caught her elbow. 'Careful, I don't want to lose you,' and realised, in that instant, that it was true.

By the time they got back down to the car, Joanna was shivering in earnest and, while she scrambled into the car, Richard fetched a rug from the boot to tuck around them.

'Take off that sweater and put this one on,' he told her, as he switched on the car's heater. 'It's one of mine, but Mum knitted it for me and she is *not* a knitter. She made that one on-stage during a run of *Marat/Sade*, and I'm afraid the madness must have spilled over from the play.'

Joanne laughed as she pulled on the thick red sweater, and discovered that one sleeve was much longer than the other and neck was all awry. Constance Marlow and she had something in common!

As she pulled off her gloves, Richard rustled around in a bag he had dumped on the back seat, and extracted a thermos and some food. Then he relaxed in his seat and sipped the hot coffee spiced with brandy, as she fell ravenously on the food—gourmet sandwiches from the hotel kitchen.

'Mmm, this liver is nice,' she said, licking her lips.

Richard had removed his hat and sun-glasses and now his eyes closed in a brief expression of exaggerated pain. 'That liver, my dear, is pâté de foie gras with truffles.'

'Is it?' Joanna inspected it with interest. 'I'm a philistine when it comes to food. I like everything, the more the better—be it *coq au vin* or the finger-licking variety. I even adore airline food.'

'Do you?' Richard looked faintly nauseated, but also rather fascinated, as she consumed most of the food, then looked at him rather guiltily.

'Aren't you hungry? Do you want some of these?'

'I'll save them for the trip home,' he said with a grin. 'You might get peckish. I can only hope that your insatiable appetite for food is matched by your appetite for love.'

'Why?' She watched him brush away the crumbs and reach for her.

'Because that's what *I'm* hungry for.'

He kissed her, moving as close as he could with the gear-stick between them, his mouth hot and persuasive against her cool one, his breath carrying the lingering aftertaste of coffee and brandy. She closed her eyes, instantly feeling a warm sweep of contentment through her body. The slight weight of her spectacles was removed from the bridge of her nose, which was scattered with whispering kisses that flowed on to her lowered lids.

'Kiss me, I need you to kiss me . . .' The husky voice wrapped around her, as his mouth returned to hers and she obeyed without question, parting her lips to seek the answer to her own needs, sliding her arms around his neck.

They kissed for long minutes and, when she drew back for a breath, he cupped her face, his eyes glittering with a fierce promise, as he read the desire in her eyes, her soft mouth. 'Lovely, isn't it?' he whispered, leaning over the top of her as he positioned her for his darting, delving tongue, enticing hers to play exquisite games of pleasure.

'God, you taste even better than I remembered,' he

groaned roughly, his hands moving caressingly from cheek to jaw, from throat to breast. Then they were sliding up under the uneven weave of the red sweater, his fingers exciting her even through the padding of blouse and woollen jerkin. He bit her mouth delicately, as he pressed urgently into the soft mounds of flesh. 'Damn it, I wish we were somewhere alone in front of a fire and you were naked beneath me,' he laughed breathily, 'or on top of me. Joanna——'

They both became aware of the tapping at the same time, and turned dazed heads to discover a young girl's face pressed against the car window. With a moan, Joanna ducked beneath the rug, as Richard casually withdrew his hands and wound down the window.

'Richard Marlow, it *is* you!' squeaked the girl before he could speak. 'I told them it was you . . .' Muffled giggles came from somewhere behind her.

His reply was cool, but polite. 'Yes, and as you can see, I'm rather busy . . .'

Like Joanna in the playground, the girl had no intention of being fobbed off. 'Is she your current girlfriend? Is she someone I know? An actress?'

'She's a champion skier,' Richard lied beautifully.

'Oh! Can I have your autograph, then, Richard? And hers, too,' as a hurried afterthought.

'You can certainly have mine.' Joanna felt the warmth of his body lift further across hers as he reached out of the window. Her breasts ached from the pressure of his chest, the centre of her body still liquid-sweet. 'But Gerda's suffering two cracked wrists from an accident at Aspen last week.'

Joanna stuffed a hand into her mouth as she listened to the scribble, then the sound of Richard's firm goodbye, and the rapid winding-up of the window.

'It's OK, Gerda, you can come out now.'

She emerged, ruffled and flustered. 'Why did you say that about me?'

'Would you rather I'd introduced you?'

She shuddered. 'How do you bear it, the lack of privacy? I would hate it, always to be at the mercy of strangers. She sounded as if she thought she had a right to know who I was.'

'Reaching out to people is part of what I do,' Richard told her soberly. 'The heart of all acting is getting into emotional touch with others, rousing their interest, their curiosity. If you treat fans with respect, they will generally respect you, and unless you're spectacularly famous the privacy is usually there for the taking . . . sometimes it's as simple as a hat and dark-glasses and ordinary clothes, like today. One learns to live with it. You will too, in time.'

'Why should I have to live with it?' she asked, bewildered.

He gave her back her glasses and watched her put them on, then he smiled, his eyes full of a shattering soft tenderness. 'Because, silly girl, you'll be living with me. But don't worry, little blind owl, I don't doubt that you'll learn to cope!'

CHAPTER SEVEN

'My God!' Jeff Hobbs's soft profanity echoed the shock in Richard's mind, as he sat in the darkened theatre staring at the profile on the screen.

'I think I've found my Garbo,' Jeff murmured reverently. 'And to think that's in harsh light. Imagine if I *tried* to make her look good . . .'

'What the hell is *she* doing in the rushes?' Richard growled, as he watched himself enter the silent scene and the camera zoomed in for a two-shot close-up.

'We ran a test of some new film stock through the second camera while we were setting up. It's pure luck that Joanna was standing in . . . you don't look half bad yourself, either.'

Luck? Richard ignored Jeff's chuckle. He had another word for it. He watched, tense with conflicting feelings, as his snowy owl disproved his theory about delicacy not transferring to the screen. The bleached flawlessness of the harshly lit skin and fine-boned angles of Joanna's face gave it an ethereal, waif-like poignancy. The wide, velvet-brown eyes with their myopically large pupils dominated the screen, the thick lashes and brows a startling counterpoint to the silver hair.

'What a fantastic vignette for the bar scene,' Jeff said, as the delicate waif became an instant gamine with a grin to camera before she stalked off, nose in the air, leaving Richard laughing behind her. 'Can't you just see her sitting there in the hazy background, some great hulking ape draped all over her and that fantastic look of disdain on her face . . .?'

Kind of him not to mention that the on-screen disdain had been for Richard! Unfortunately, he could see it all too clearly—Joanna's slight body dressed up in some garish, tacky dress, a street-toughened waif who despised the men she lived off. The combination of sex and fragility would be dynamite.

The image, once fixed in his brain, wouldn't leave him. Professional instincts battled with personal ones. Any other woman, and Richard knew that he would have been pounding at her door, contract in hand. But this wasn't any woman. This was *his* woman.

Since Egmont she had been trying to avoid him, but Richard had been pleased, rather than disappointed. It meant that she was vulnerable, and knew it. She had chosen to take his remarks about her living with him as a joke, but his experienced ear had detected the hidden trace of panic in her laughter. She *wanted* to take him seriously, but she was afraid to, so she was pretending to herself, and to him, that the very idea was impossibly ridiculous. It wasn't and soon she would know it, too. Until then, he didn't want anything to distract her. She was his own private intimate discovery and he didn't intend to share her ... not yet, anyway.

God, Marlow, listen to yourself! Richard closed his eyes, ignoring the colour tests on the screen, appalled at his hypocrisy and arrogance. She wasn't his ... she wasn't anyone's ... she was herself. He had always believed in a woman's right to self-determination, yet here he was actually acting like the archetypal paternalistic, chauvinistic pig! Making decisions about her future that he had no right to make, contemplating denying her the chance, however small it might be, to pursue the very same dreams that had brought him fame, fortune and artistic fulfilment. How dare he!

He was jealous. God, he was actually jealous of *himself*, if such a thing were possible. Jealous of what the public Richard Marlow could offer the woman the private Richard loved, afraid it would change her, take her away from him. Hadn't he smugly told himself that he wanted to free her to soar? And yet here he was thinking of caging her in restrictions for entirely selfish reasons. No! He worked himself up into a fury of self-contempt: he would give her her chance! He would prove to both of them that he was capable of rising above selfish considerations, of rejecting this sudden, embarrassing excess of primitive macho possessiveness. He would share his snowy owl if it killed him!

Joanna was still yawning as she answered the door. She choked on the yawn, jumping back as Richard swept majestically past her, clutching the lapels of her robe together as she remembered the last time she had confronted him in her pyjamas.

She stared at him as he glared out of the window. *Now* what was the problem? Aside from him, of course! It wasn't fair that he affected her like this, when poor Duncan, whom she'd known and liked for years, couldn't raise a spark. Duncan had rung for a chat the evening of her visit to the ski fields and their comfortable conversation had filled her with guilt. She couldn't contemplate marrying him now, not when it appeared that she was so susceptible to other men ... even men who blithely suggested a live-in affair with the same casualness that other people used to ask whether you wanted milk or sugar in your coffee! It would be funny if it wasn't so ... offensive.

'How would you like a part in the bar scene.' He suddenly spun around and stared broodingly at her, making it a statement not a question. 'We got some accidental footage of you when you were standing in for Becky. You're as photogenic as she is.'

It sounded like an accusation. 'Is that what you woke me up for, to tell me I'm photogenic?' she asked, testily.

'No! I was just explaining why I wanted you for the scene,' he said impatiently. 'It's not a speaking part but——'

'Thanks, but no thanks,' Joanna interrupted him. 'Now, can I go back to sleep?'

'You're refusing?' He didn't look upset, probably because he didn't believe her, she thought crankily.

'Yes, I'm refusing. This is probably another of your little personal character tests. Well, paranoids can never be convinced that they're wrong, so I'm not even going to bother to try. If you want to believe that I'm some conniving little tart——'

'Conniving, never! But you'd make a very luscious tart.' Her crankiness seemed to smooth the thunderous brow, and he gave her a whimsical smile. 'In fact, that's what I want you to be. Will you play the tart for me, darling?'

'Go away Richard, I'm sick of your silly games.' Her own brow rumpled as she crossed her arms firmly over her chest.

'I'm serious——'

'So am I.' If he was, it only made her more determined not to be coaxed, teased or coerced.

'Look, darling, it's just a tiny cameo, you'll enjoy it. And you won't have to move, if that's what's worrying you.' He descibed the part with a vivid enthusiasm that aroused her reluctant admiration, but it didn't change her mind. 'It's the kind of little touch that gives a film depth,' he concluded persuasively. 'And who knows what it might lead to for you? Think how impressed your students would be to see you in a movie.'

'I don't do things just to impress people, Richard,' she said crushingly. 'That's your speciality. God knows, I've told you often enough I'm not interested in acting. I thought you understood, but obviously not.' She wasn't a real person to him, she thought bitterly, just a supporting member of the cast allotted only the needs and desires that he ascribed to her. He had almost fooled her, on that lovely afternoon in the snow, into thinking he was genuinely interested in what she thought and did. Why, she had almost wished . . . She glared at him, and his smile faded completely. He put his hands on his hips and planted his feet astride.

'Damn it, Joanna, I don't go around offering roles like this to all and sundry. It's perfect for you. You should be flattered!'

'Please, keep your voice down or you'll wake Becky.' Joanna used the excuse to move away from his disturbing nearness and close the door to the bedroom. 'She needs the extra sleep after filming last night. Of course I'm flattered, Richard, knowing how possessive you are about your film——'

Her sarcastic stress on the word possessive seemed to strike a sensitive chord. He stiffened, his chin lifting and eyes narrowing . . . sure signs of idling temper.

'——but I don't see why I should do it, just because it's what *you* want——'

'What *I* want?' He glared at her, looking magnificently fierce, but Joanna wasn't afraid. She was exhilarated, and a little amused at his loss of cool. 'I'm not doing this for myself Joanna. I'm doing this for *your* sake . . .'

Her incredulous laugh made him realise how ludicrous the statement was after his earlier enthusiasm, and a touch of colour brushed the high cheekbones.

'Well, yes, of course *I* want you for the film, but it's only a minor part in a minor scene, and it's no skin off my nose if you won't do it. But you . . .'

Joanna stared at him blankly, totally bewildered. If it was all so minor, what on earth was the fuss about? Why did her refusal just make him seem more grimly determined to change her mind?

'Damn it, woman, you're not even listening to me!' he roared.

Joanna blinked. 'Not when you shout, no. And I told you, Becky——'

'Damn Becky! And damn you! And will you stop saying no all the time!'

She set her spectacles straight on her small nose, savouring the pause. 'No.' She smiled primly at him. 'No. No. No.' He opened his mouth. 'And, no!'

There was a heavy silence. The green eyes simmered with sultry darkness. Joanna held the stare: angry young males took the slightest waver as weakness. He broke first, turning aside with an explosive curse.

'You're impossible, do you know that? Impossible! Stubborn! Short-sighted, pig-headed . . .' He swung around suddenly and pointed a dramatic finger at her. 'Don't think I don't know what you're trying to do here, Joanna. You're doing this deliberately, aren't you, to get your own back?' He began to pace angrily as he spoke, jabbing an occasional finger in her direction. 'You're trying to provoke me into having a fight. You want barriers to hide behind. You want to make me so angry that I'll say something unforgivable and storm off in a huff. It's not going to work, Joanna. I'm not angry. After all, it's totally your decision.' The increasing staccato of each succeeded syllable gave the lie to his words. 'The fact that *I* think it's a totally *wrong* decision doesn't matter. It's not going to change anything between us, nothing! Do you hear me?'

'I should, you're shouting again,' she said sweetly. 'You handle rejection just as arrogantly as you handle everything else, so of course nothing will change. I'm sure your little film might be a success, even if you don't have everything exactly how you want it. If not, well, there's always the next one . . .'

He went up, as she knew he would, in a murderous flash of green.

'*Little* film? *Might?* My God, at that rate there wouldn't *be* a next one. You don't have much faith in me, do you, Joanna? No wonder you're so determined to fend me off. Who wants to be associated with a failure? Of course, I'm so slick and superficial that it wouldn't matter to *me*——'

'I'm sure it would, Richard,' she heaped a few more coals on the fire and stood back to admire the sparks flying skywards, 'but you'd bounce back. You always do. You could always go back to acting . . . I'm sure your father would——'

'I'm not washed up yet, you cold-hearted bitch!' He gave her a look that would have seared asbestos and, forgetting his earlier analysis of her motives, now proven beyond doubt, he slammed out of the suite.

What on earth was *that* all about? Joanna wondered as she went back through the bedroom to take a shower. It had been weird behaviour, even for Richard. Had the offer been another line in his seduction routine, or had it been his idea of a tacit gesture of trust? Either way, they were as far apart in expectations and misconceptions as they had ever been. And to make that ludicrous suggestion that he was doing it for *her* sake. That relegated her to the level of a starstruck teenager!

The sad fact was that he had been right about the barriers. But she didn't need to create them, they were there already. And the biggest of them was that, even if she didn't marry Duncan, even if she remained a spinster for the rest of her life, she still couldn't picture herself embarking on the kind of casual, physical love affair that Richard was obviously used to. And conducting it in full view of the public eye, to boot.

It was a difficult day for everyone. On-set, Richard was impossible to please but frigidly polite and, typically, didn't attempt to hide the source of his displeasure, saving his chilliest of looks for Joanna. She ignored him, revising her opinion that he didn't sulk.

She wasn't going to let him make her feel guilty just because she wouldn't fit in neatly with his plans, she told herself as she got ready for dinner that evening. With a late morning call for the following day, Becky had decided that she could bear to tear herself away from her fascinating new life for one night, and was sleeping over at her schoolfriend Sandra's place. So Joanna wouldn't have her niece as buffer and, when she entered the restaurant, her heart sank. Richard was at the head of the long table, and the only empty chair was beside him. Reserved for her? Meeting the challenging green gaze over the heads of the other diners, Joanna was certain of it. She inhaled deeply. Well, she would walk on to his damned stage set and put on a brilliant performance of a woman who didn't give a fig for his opinion!

She had got within melting distance of that hard, hot stare when suddenly Finn appeared at her elbow, and she found herself carried off to a corner table for two. Finn bowed mockingly in Richard's direction and sat down, grinning.

'Always fancied myself as the Scarlet Pimpernel.' He set up the drinks with his customary speed, and then asked cosily, 'What crime have you committed this time, Joanna? Before you speak, let me assure you that everything you say will be taken down and used to settle bets. I have been delegated by the rabble to adjudicate.'

Why not? Let Richard look the fool for once. 'I refused a part in his film.'

'What an insult!' Finn regarded her with acute delight. 'Although I do have some sympathy with Richard, I saw those rushes, too. Regretting it already?'

'Definitely not. I don't want to be an actress.'

'Lucky Richard,' Finn murmured under his breath, and gave her a smouldering smile. 'Then smile, *show* him you're not regretting it. I love your dress, violet suits you. Did I ever tell you about the time . . .?'

His tall tales kept her amused, interspersed with

occasional updates on what Richard was doing, so she wouldn't have to give in to the almost irresistible urge to turn around to see. To try and bolster her pride, she defiantly munched her way through four courses and made heavy inroads into Finn's red wine. She also had a second Irish coffee, made to Finn's own, very potent, patriotic recipe.

'He's scintillating,' he told her, as she sipped the heady brew. 'Have you ever noticed how Richard scintillates when he's pretending not to be furious? Well, at the moment he positively hurts the eyes. Wait—he's getting up—is he coming over here?' Joanna felt a breathless flutter in her chest which subsided abruptly as Finn continued his commentary. 'No, he's walking over to the door, limping with great flair, I might add, and the head held high—pride and pathos. You can't help but admire his exits, can you? I always said that Richard could make an exit look like an entrance to some even greater scene ...'

Joanna smiled hollowly, feeling oddly deflated. She hadn't wanted a confrontation, had she? So why did she feel cheated?

'Hell, isn't it?' Finn said softly, as he watched the brown eyes flicker behind the magnifying glass.

'What?' she asked absently, the dregs of coffee and alcohol suddenly bitter on her tongue.

'Love.' Her eyes went to him in shock, but he was studying his cup, and the protest died on her lips as she really looked at him for the first time that evening. The grooves on the handsome, ravaged face seemed deeper tonight, the eyes dark and bitter as the coffee. Black shadow was beginning to show on his chin and his mouth had a grim, to-hell-with-it twist. Here she had sat, full of her own petty concerns, when Finn, too, looked like a soul in need of rescue.

He smiled humourlessly when he looked up and saw the expression on her face. 'She walked out on me, did you know? Of course you didn't, best kept secret in Hollywood ... She was afraid that if it came out it might really put the skids under my career . . . or maybe she was afraid it might contaminate hers.' Bianca, he was talking about Bianca, Joanna realised, and sensed that here was the reason for the bitterness of his moods, the 'other problems' that Richard had mentioned. 'Told me she was leaving me the day she went to Paris. Said she wasn't coming back unless I shaped up. Said I had to choose—her or the booze. Hell of a choice for an Irishman, huh?' He poured another slug of whiskey into his coffee, from the bottle that he ordered the waiter to leave on the table. He smiled with the same kind of defiance that had tinged Joanna's earlier gaiety. 'Know what the last thing she said to me was? She loved me.' He laughed sourly. 'Loved me, but couldn't live with me the way I was. Great line, huh? Bianca always makes great exits, too. She and Richard both, damn him for an interfering swine. She'd been crying on his shoulder, and good old Rich isn't a guy to miss a chance at playing white knight.' Another whiskey sloshed the sides of the cup. 'Always drank hard, never bothered her before. Says she loves me and walks out. Can you figure that? Typical bloody woman—wants to be equal but hasn't got the guts to fight on equal terms . . . just . . . walks out.' He focused his black bitterness suddenly on Joanna. 'You women, you want it all ways. When the going's good you're all sugar and spice but, when things get rough, you melt away. No bloody stamina, that's your problem. No stamina . . .'

At any other time Joanna would have listened compassionately, let him spew out all the poison, knowing that she was just a handy ear, but she was still smarting from her own sense of injustice against the male sex. Suddenly, she was mad enough to take issue with the slur on womankind, even if it meant that she was obliquely defending the other woman in the case, the woman who had jilted Richard, who obviously made a habit of walking out on the men she professed to love.

That must have been how she ended up in Finn's suite, matching him glass for glass, vodka straight for whiskey on the rocks, intent on proving that a woman's stamina was even greater than a man's. It was dumb, juvenile and what was more, if Finn was an alcoholic, it was positively criminal, but Joanna felt reckless. Reckless enough, and confident enough, to issue him a challenge that he was just drunk enough to accept—if she could outdrink him, he would give up the booze.

'What the hell!' he roared. 'I was going to do it, anyway. But if you lose . . .' He wagged a playful finger at her. 'If *you* lose, darlin', you gotta go on bended knees to His Lordship and beg for that part after all . . . deal?'

'Deal,' Joanna had declared, deciding there and then that ethics had no part in a drinking contest. She would cheat. Demeaning herself to Richard was totally unthinkable!

The minutes blurred into an hour or more, as Joanna surreptitiously fed the pot plant at her elbow, in between cautious sips to deflect suspicion. She didn't think that Finn was in any condition to notice her discreet arm actions, but when he suddenly grabbed her she gave a shriek, thinking that he had caught her red-handed. But Finn's mind was on another track entirely.

'You wouldn't walk out on a man if you really loved 'im, would you, J'anna? I bet you wouldn'.' He sighed as he slumped heavily against her, his shaggy head hitting her ear, a whole glassful of whiskey tipping down the front of her dress. Joanna shrieked again at the cold and shoved at him. He fell back clumsily, dragging her with him off the couch on to the floor. Joanna's hand was trapped beneath his dead weight and she squirmed on top of him, trying to get it free.

'Finn, for goodness sake——'

'Wassamatter? Bianca . . .?' he mumbled thickly, his hand tangling in the loose neckline of her dress so that when she jerked away the fabric was dragged off her shoulder.

'Finn!' Joanna shuddered as she felt some of the whiskey run down between her breasts and pool in her navel, God, if anyone walked in on them now . . .

'Is this a private orgy or can anyone join in?'

Joanna froze. Finn took a few seconds longer to react, shaking his head like a shaggy dog before glaring blearily up at Richard, leaning indolently on his stick in the doorway.

'You should make sure your door is closed properly, Finn,' he drawled at his electrified audience, 'before you start making adulterous moves. Imagine if I had been someone with a penchant for taking photos. As for you, Joanna,' he transferred a grave, sad-eyed look to her flushed face, 'I'm deeply disappointed in you ...'

'This——' Joanna wrenched out of Finn's grip and scrabbled to her feet, hitching up her damp dress as she did so, feeling guilty as if she and Finn had actually been ... She gulped, 'This really isn't what it looks like, Richard——'

'Isn't it?' The sad, cynical eyes dipped, and Joanna followed his gaze to see the wet fabric clinging to her small breasts, moulding the cold, hard nipples with embarrassing frankness. She clapped an arm across her chest, blushing furiously, and Richard raised his eyes to say blandly, 'It *looks* as though Finn got drunk and pounced on you in a fit of maudlin self-pity, and you fell on the floor trying to fight him off. But if, as you tell me, that's not what happened, perhaps I ought to make my excuses and withdraw gracefully.'

Joanna's mouth hung open, the wind whipped from her sails, and Finn, shambling upright, growled, 'Yeah, why don't you? J'anna and I are doin' just fine, aren't we, darlin'?'

Joanna ignored him, staring at Richard, suddenly seeing the spark in his eyes, the suspicious straightness of his mouth. Why ... he was *amused*! He thought it was funny!—finding her and Finn in a clinch on the floor. Why? Because he didn't believe that any man would seriously make a pass at her? *He* had.

'So why don't you just butt out, sonny boy,' said Finn belligerently. 'And keep your bloody nose out of my affairs.'

'Because I don't think that Joanna wants an affair . . . at least, not with *you*,' Richard had the gall to drawl and Joanna began to blush all over again, but not with embarrassment. How dare he stand there and silently laugh! How dare he imply in that offensively arrogant manner that the only man she would want an affair with was himself! And how *dare* he claim to 'think' that he might be falling in love with her and yet not even have the decency to show a scrap of jealousy! Not that she would have expected him to challenge Finn to a duel, but he might have at least shouted a bit. 'Do you want me to butt out, Joanna?' he was asking, eyes dancing knowingly.

'Yes, she does!' Finn roared, defending her pride with his alcohol-fuelled temper. 'F'your information J'anna and I unnerstand each other. We make a good team . . . we were just getting started, weren' we, darlin'?'

Richard's eyebrows rose in amusement, until he suddenly noticed the glass on the floor and the other on the table by the pot plant, and the two opened, half-empty bottles. The humour vanished completely, replaced by a look of hard interrogation that had Joanna swallowing nervously, and now, perversely, wishing for the return of that mocking smile.

'We were . . . we were just . . .' She faltered weakly under the green contempt.

'She holds her liquor better'n you do these days, ole boy,' said Finn slyly, slinging an unwelcome arm across Joanna's slim shoulders. 'She doesn' preach me sanctimonious lectures. We got a bet running, she and I, to see who passes out first . . .'

It sounded indefensible, and Joanna wasn't surprised when Richard hit the roof. 'Of all the stupid, senseless, idiotic, childish——!' he yelled at her guilty, downbent head. She knew she deserved the litany, and was about to admit it when Finn again steamed to the rescue. With a low roar he launched himself at Richard. Joanna raised her head just in time to see the wild swing miss Richard's jaw by a mile, carry on, hang suspended for a moment in the air and then follow the rest of him bonelessly to the floor.

'Congratulations,' said Richard. 'I think you just won your bet.'

'I . . . we . . . he said he'd give up drinking if I won,' she said feebly.

'And you believed him?' His voice rose incredulously. 'No, don't answer that, I didn't come looking for you to talk about Finn. He can look after himself. I suppose you're totally bombed, too?'

'My body has a very high tolerance for alcohol,' she said loftily.

'You're not the slightest bit drunk?' he asked sceptically, and she shook her head vigorously. A fresh gleam entered his eyes, and he took her hand and led her to the door. 'Let's find out, shall we?'

What was he going to do, breath-test her? 'We can't just leave. What about Finn——?'

'Finn has slept on many a less comfortable floor, believe me,' said Richard as he steered her imperiously down the hallway. 'I've even shared some of them with him in my time.'

'But——'

'But, nothing, Joanna. Sobering up has to be his decision. He has to want to or his promises are just so much hot air. Don't kid yourself that you can make the difference. There's only one person who has a chance in hell, and that's Bianca. At the moment, for Finn, all women are unsatisfactory substitutes for Bianca.'

'You don't seem to have much sympathy for someone who's supposed to be your friend,' Joanna said, stung by the thought that for Richard, too, she might be just a substitute. 'Maybe you don't care if he stays sober or not. Maybe you want Bianca to leave him, the way she left you. Maybe you want her back because you're still in love with her!'

He laughed with offensive delight as he flung open the door to his suite and hustled her protestingly inside, leaning back against the closed door again and grabbing the soft fabric of her belt to anchor her still, as she would have slid angrily away.

'Listen, my jealous darling—the last thing that Finn needs is sympathy. He's a hell-raiser from way back and he's just facing the unpalatable fact that in future he's going to have to raise hell sober or live without the woman he loves ... the woman who loves him.'

'I'm not jealous,' Joanna interrupted fiercely, trying to ignore the way that her body nestled disturbingly against his. Maybe she was a bit drunk, after all. '*You* weren't.' She closed her eyes when she realised what she had blurted out. She *was* drunk. She felt his warm bubble of laughter against her averted cheek.

'Because, contrary to all the PR hype, Finn is a faithful husband and you, my dear, don't tremble when he touches you ... the way you do when *I* touch you.' He proved it with a caress that both infuriated and excited her, and he laid firm fingers against her lips when she would have protested. 'No, shut up and listen, you infuriating woman, and don't pretend you're not interested. The reason that Finn is mad at me is not because he thinks I'm having it away with his wife, but because I "betrayed" him by siding with her over his drinking. She came to me when she reached the end of her tolerance, and I agreed that it was time to cry enough. She loves him too much to stay and watch him destroy himself for no good reason. Sure, there are younger talents breathing down his neck and sure, he's made one or two flops in the last couple of years, a few wrong choices, but he's a great actor and that's something that no one else can take away from him. Only he can do that, if he pickles his brain, but I don't think Bianca's going to let him. If this doesn't work she'll try something even more drastic—she's a hell of a woman.' He saw the suspicion spread in the wide brown eyes, and admonished the doubt by sliding an arm around behind Joanna's waist and jerking her more tightly against him, letting his stick fall unnoticed to the floor.

'We were never in love—never. Bianca and I had a very

brief fling a long time ago, when we first met, but that was over before she ever met Finn. The engagement thing was just studio hype, they thought a hot romance would help the première. We went along with it because neither of us were otherwise involved at the time and then, when she and Finn discovered instant chemistry, we kept it up as a cover, a bit of fun at the Press's expense. Only unfortunately Finn, who always wants to go one better, had this great idea that they would sneak off to Reno and cock a snook at everyone by getting married, and that's where they were when I had the crash. When no loving fiancée turned up to hold my shattered hand at the hospital, some Press-hound smelt a rat and went hunting, and then the whole pack were in full cry. When that happens you can "no comment", and deny, and "just good friends" until the cows come home, and still open the papers next day to banner headlines and the "full facts" you didn't tell them. We couldn't very well confess— the best way to make an enemy of a reporter is to tell him you've used him for your own ends—so we decided the best thing to do was sit tight until the story died, which it did eventually . . . as much as a Hollywood gossip story *can* die. So, Joanna——' His other hand let go of her belt and stroked up to lightly encircle her throat, his fingers cool against her heated skin. '. . . Now that you know I'm not a callous, vengeful, wife-stealing swine, are you going to stop fluffing your feathers at me, little owl, and let me into your soft, dark, body-warm nest . . .?'

CHAPTER EIGHT

THE soft, dark, warm words burrowed deep into her defences.

'Let me go, Richard,' she said weakly, tilting her head back to frown up into his face. It was a mistake. Now she saw the tender plea in his eyes and the sensual softness of his mouth. She became even more aware of her breasts, tight against the rapid rise of his chest, her thighs somehow insinuated between his braced legs so that their hips fitted naturally together. She closed her eyes hoping that by shutting out the sight of him she would find the strength to resist, but her other senses ambushed her with overwhelming force.

'If you think that after this morning . . . today . . . you can——' she began desperately.

'Ah, yes, this morning,' he interrupted her with such grave, husky penitence that her eyes flew open just in time to absorb the exquisite warmth of his rueful smile. His hand stroked up through the cropped silk of her hair until he was cupping the back of her small skull, holding her still to receive his penance. 'What can I say about this morning? I'm thoroughly ashamed of myself. I went temporarily crazy and then compounded it by sulking. I'm sorry. I was really furious with myself, not with you. You see, my first thought was not to let you get within ten feet of a camera because I wanted you as part of my personal life, not my professional one. I was disgusted with myself so I tore over to you intent on impressing upon us both that I wasn't a selfish swine and ended up being even more selfish. What I *meant* by saying I was doing it for you, was that I was doing it for *us*. Showing that you were free to choose. Whatever you want to do is fine with me—act or don't act—I realised during my sulks that it didn't matter. Whatever you do you're still Joanna, and to tell the truth I suppose if you'd reacted in any other way I would have been disappointed. That's one of the reasons I went crazy . . . you make me feel that I don't know myself as well as I thought I did.

'I'm not quite sure how to behave with you, how to reach you. But at least I don't *think* I'm in love with you any more . . .' With satisfaction, he felt the faint tremor of shocked regret that shot through her small bones. 'I *know* I am; and I'm going to prove it to you. I wish there was time to take pleasure in a slow wooing, darling, but there isn't . . . so trust me . . . let me make love to you now and show you how

I feel, how I can make *you* feel . . .'

'Because no one refuses the great romantic actor's seduction routine?' whispered Joanna shakily, fighting a losing battle with herself. Richard, pleading, with soft words and kisses . . .

'No . . . because you can't help yourself,' he murmured in her ear, as he tasted the small lobe.

'But I can . . .' she lied huskily, shifting restlessly against him.

'Then help me . . . help *me*,' he groaned softly in erotic plea, releasing his hold on her head and body to pull her hands from his shoulders down over his chest, sliding her fingers between the buttons so that she could feel the contrasts of soft, springy hair and hot satin skin. She could feel the thunder of his heart, too, against her fingertips as he kissed her mouth at last, and she conceded a limited defeat. A few kisses couldn't hurt . . . no one could call this voluptuous pleasure pain . . .

One long, slow kiss blended into another, and another . . . Slowly, slowly, without her being aware of it, Richard drew Joanna across the room in a swaying, sensual dance and into the dimly lit bedroom. On the journey his loose white cotton shirt became unbuttoned, the better to feel the softly stroking hands exploring the muscled hardness. His hands linked in the small of her back, drawing the supple bow of her body against the hard shaft of his loins, encouraging the flex of her hips as he eased a long, lean thigh between her legs with each small step of their progress.

It was only when she felt the firm press of the bed against the back of her knees that Joanna realised where a few kisses had led her, and she stiffened. Richard lifted his head.

'Joanna——' His eyes were slumberous green, half closed, his mouth passionately soft as he set out to conquer her weak resistance. '. . . You're damp——' His hand came up to trace the curving dip of her neckline. '——and you smell like a distillery . . . shouldn't we take this off before the Revenue Men arrive?'

Joanna blinked at him, disarmed by the teasing sensuousness of his smile, the light-heartedness of the enticement. Was this what loving Richard would be like—kisses and smiles and the intoxication of being cherished, desired, above all other women . . .? He could make her want to laugh, even as he made her want him, desperately.

'Don't be afraid,' he murmured, still with a teasing lilt, 'I'll hide you in my arms. You'll never want for an illicit thrill with me: "I know the ways of pleasure, the sweet strains, The lullings and the relishes of it; The propositions of hot blood and brains . . ."'

His mouth covered her shivering gasp with a devouring hunger that consumed her amusement and the rags of her common sense, stunning her yet again with the swift transition from teasing to intense passion. He used words the same way he was using his mouth and hands—to caress, to seduce, to delight . . . Joanna felt the unhurried slide of the zip at the back of her dress from shoulder-blade to buttocks with a rush of feverish anticipation, as if her emotions were being unzipped along with her body.

Kissing her, he unbuckled her belt and let it fall with a soft thump to the floor and then slid the violet jersey-knit from her shoulders, following it to the floor as he knelt to take off her shoes and coloured tights. Only then did he tilt his head to look up at her with such an expression of aroused satisfaction that Joanna's mouth went dry and she clenched her hands in the tousled flame of his hair to tug him to his feet. He rose with leisurely ease, pressing his lips to the soft pale skin of her thighs, the hard points of her narrow hips under their lavender lace, the silk of her flat stomach, the slope of her shoulders, the curve of her throat and finally, with a small fierce groan, her mouth. Her elbows resting on his shoulders, fingers still buried in his hair, Joanna clung to him, a tiny distracted part of her brain mourning that he had skipped her breasts . . . probably hadn't even noticed them, and yet he had made them ache unbearably. She was mad, utterly mad—as mad as he was! Why was she letting him do this, enjoying it so passionately, her body singing so sweetly to his song . . .?

Without breaking the kiss he pressed her gently down on to the crisp, turned-back sheets of the bed, not releasing her mouth until they were both breathless. He half sat then, body curved towards her, and instinctively Joanna let her hands fall to cover her breasts.

He clicked his tongue softly. 'Silly owl, don't hide from me. I've seen them before, remember?'

She flushed and turned her face away, cooling her cheek against the pillow, her body tensing with fear this time, not desire. If he teased her now . . .

'Sweet and small and perfect . . .' The soft, worshipful words sent a hot tingling shock through her nervous system, and she heard him chuckle. '. . . And so very, very sensitive. May I kiss your lovely breasts, Joanna?'

Still flushed she looked at him, his mouth warm and moist, and imagined the tongue nestled in the moistness and what it would do . . . She flushed more deeply, her skin glowing with confusion and he laughed softly and bent and tasted her, delicately, assessingly, closing his eyes with pleasure as her nipple flowered between his tongue and palate.

'Mmmm, you taste of whiskey,' he approved huskily, as he looped his hands under her shoulder-blades to lift her to his mouth. 'I could get drunk on your breasts, darling . . . and stay drunk, for the rest of my life . . .'

Gracefully, he sank over her on the bed and began to make love to her little breasts with such enthusiastic fervour that Joanna felt that she had died and gone to some sweet heaven of the senses. Why, if this was making love, hadn't she done it long before now? Why had she waited? Was it for this . . .? For this man . . .? He made her feel . . . like a 38C! She laughed dreamily up at the white ceiling, her hands moving reverently over the shifting muscles of his back and he looked up at the sound, and smiled at her smile, and turned on his side to cup her head and draw it to his chest.

'. . . Now you . . .'

The soft command made her tremble. Could she really make him feel the things that she was feeling? Could she wield such power ... even with so little experience? Wonderingly, she opened her mouth against his salty skin and discovered that the taste was addictive. The hands cupping her head shook as his body hardened under her eager ministrations and he no longer needed to guide her. His arousal perfumed his skin, flavoured it, stimulated her appetite—until with a harsh groan he rolled away from her.

'I need more than this, I want to feel you against me,' he said thickly, as he stood to pull off his tight, black jeans. As he hooked his thumbs into his thin, black silk briefs, he gave her a smile of sultry confidence. 'I want you to see me, too. I hope I don't disappoint you.'

How could he, when she had nothing to compare him with? I should tell him that, she thought half-heartedly, but if he knows I'm a virgin he might stop, might feel compelled to act nobly. She had forgotten all about her foolproof scheme to defend himself against his lovemaking by throwing out ideas for his film. Right now, there were no ideas in her head but those he had placed there ... ideas of love, passion, desire, fulfilment.

'I've already seen you,' she said breathlessly, unselfconscious in her semi-nudity as she watched his unveiling, '... in the movies.'

'And did you like what you saw?' he asked gravely, discarding the briefs.

'I ... I'm not a voyeur at heart,' she said, unable to take her eyes off him. She certainly hadn't seen *this* much! He was so beautiful, lean-muscled, svelte-hipped but male, oh, so male ... and he wanted her, badly ...

'You're certainly giving a good imitation of one,' he said, frankly enjoying her eyes on him as he moved back to the bed. 'It's all simulated, you know, on screen. It's difficult to get genuinely aroused when thirty people are breathing down your neck, no matter how attractive your co-star. And you can't choose your co-stars. You can, however,

choose your lovers . . . and I choose you, Joanna Carson . . .'
His voice dipped in erotic promise as he stood before her.

'You're incredible,' said Joanna, automatically responding to the masculine arrogance, but it didn't come out
sarcastically, and she wasn't looking at his face. To his
astonishment, Richard felt himself blush. God, she was
looking at him as if she'd never seen a man before, with a
mixture of awe and arousal that set the blood pounding in
his already painfully engorged loins. Behind her glasses the
big owl-eyes widened and he felt himself getting out of
control.

'Damn it, Joanna, if you don't stop looking at me like
that I'm going to embarrass myself in a way that I haven't
done since I was a randy teenager,' he said in roughly
sensual threat as he came back down to her.

'What?' she asked, startled into naïveté by the hint of
desperation in his voice, and the sudden electric contact of
skin on skin.

'Do you really need me to explain?' he chuckled huskily,
as he knelt astride her and placed his hands possessively on
her hips.

She realised what he had meant and closed her eyes
briefly at her own foolishness—only to arch in gasping
shock as he lowered himself slowly against her, centring his
arousal against the lavender lace, enjoying the mutual
excitement of temporary frustration. He rocked himself
languidly back and forth, bending to sip her small moans
from her lips, his hands completely cupping her taut
breasts, moving in rhythm with the rest of his body so that
the small, hard peaks slid between his fingers and were
trapped in an exquisite friction.

She was still wearing her glasses, but he made no move to
take them off. They added a certain piquancy to her
nudity, and he wanted her to see very clearly what he was
doing to her, and what she was doing to him. Lovemaking
was a feast for all the senses and Richard intended that his
little owl be thoroughly sated. Later, when they made love
again, he would take them off and satisfy another fantasy, a

disturbingly macho one that he was vaguely embarrassed to admit to—to have her helpless in his bed, gloriously reliant on him, blindly following his instruction ... he would have her braille his body, guide her through the moves that she might not be able to see clearly, but which she would feel with stunning intensity. It would be like making love to two women, two Joannas, both his. He closed his eyes and shuddered with the dual pleasure of fact and fantasy ...

When the telephone rang neither heard it at first, but the soft burr beside the bed insisted and, with a curse, Richard lent over to knock the receiver to the floor. He turned back, to the accompaniment of a squawk. 'Richard? Richard? *Richard*, pick up this phone *at once!*' The last, drilling phrase was a masterpiece of projection. Richard froze.

'Oh, my God, I don't believe it!' An arm still clamping Joanna to his side, he stretched to scoop up the receiver to his ear. 'Mother?'

Mother? Joanna was shocked out of her sensual cocoon and into a state of intense embarrassment. She tried to squirm out of Richard's grip but he held on tightly, nestling the telephone receiver into the crook of his neck so that his hand was free to caress her soothingly.

'. . . Yes, you did as a matter of fact,' he was saying with a grin, 'but no doubt it's for a good reason ... it had *better* be good.' He winked at Joanna and for an awful instant she thought he was going to tell his mother exactly what she had interrupted. 'Before you say anything, though, I ought to tell you that I'm fully cast—unless you want to play an ageing street-walker——' He jerked his ear from the resultant blast with a laugh, while Joanna slapped at his roving hand. My God, he was talking to his mother and trying to make love at the same time; had the man no decency? He was joking, enjoying the situation, apparently not the least eager to hurry the conversation along. Perhaps he was used to breaking up life into a series of takes, as he did with his films. Well, Joanna wasn't. Her mood was completely destroyed.

She pulled herself away from him, ignoring the indulgent look he gave her. He was even still *aroused!* What kind of sexual athlete—or pervert—could sustain his arousal through a light-hearted chat with his mother, for goodness sake? Joanna jumped off the bed as if it was scalding hot and looked frantically around for the lavender panties which had mysteriously shed themselves along with her inhibitions. She put them on, and her dress, with indecent haste. Of course, Constance Marlow couldn't see through the telephone but Joanna felt wretchedly exposed. *Constance Marlow.* His mother was famous. The whole damned family was extraordinary—not at all the kind of people that Joanna would fit in with. Next to them she must seem less than insignificant. Richard called her an owl and made it an endearment but, like all nicknames, it contained some truth. Next to the bright plumage of the birds who flocked in his brilliant, sunlit world she must seem rather dull. Once he had got his quirky obsession with making love to her out of his system, his brief flare of interest would fade quickly. Joanna was conscious of a hollow, empty ache as she looked at the handsome, mobile face lit with warm amusement. She could never hope to hold that quicksilver interest for long, and though desire for him still vibrated in her very bones, she had to be strong. There were only five days of filming left. For Richard that might be enough, but Joanna was a for-ever-after girl. His protestations of love she took with a wagon-load of salt. The kind of love that flared so quickly and so fiercely bright soon consumed itself to ashes.

'Is she? When? Well, of course I will!' He was laughing, stretched out naked on the rumpled bed, obviously delighted at what his mother was saying. *She?* A new prospect perhaps, a new challenge? 'Yes I will, I'll give her such a good time she might finally decide I'm the better man after all ... as long as she returns the favour in her usual style ... or should I say flavour!'

Joanna slammed the door viciously behind her. Let him laugh that off with his mother! In her room, she wallowed in a deliciously tearful sense of miserable martyrdom until the inevitable, imperious knock.

'Joanna? It's me, let me in.'

The big bad wolf. Not by the hair of my chinny chin chin, thought Joanna as she wadded a sodden tissue, disgusted at her cowardice.

'Joanna? Come on, darling, I know you're in there. I'm sorry about the call, but you shouldn't have run away. Come on, open up!' Thump, thump.

She edged closer, drawn by a force stronger than her will.

'Now, Joanna . . .' The coaxing drawl that she so loved and hated brought her up short. She wasn't going to let herself be seduced all over again!

'Go away, Richard. I'm tired, and I've had too much to drink.'

Silence. If she strained she could imagine the sound of his breathing through the solid wood. She touched the door, then snatched her hand back when he spoke.

'It's too late for excuses, my dear. You don't get drunk, remember? You wanted it as much as I did, drink or no drink.'

'It was a mistake, Richard. It just wouldn't work, we . . . I . . . I don't want to get involved with anything that I can't handle. *Please* go away.' She closed her eyes. That last, inadvertent plea had sounded far too desperate.

He must have thought so too, because amusement tempered his impatience. 'I dare you to open this door and tell me to go away to my face . . . Joanna? . . . At least open the door. You can't hide in there for ever, you know.'

She did know. 'I don't want to talk about it. Go away and stop harassing me, I'm not listening any more.'

She went into the bathroom and closed the door, loudly. Then she turned on the shower, and the basin taps for good measure. With the serpent's voice drowned out, she sat down on the closed toilet seat to review her situation. It looked pretty hopeless. Admit it, Joanna, if you're not already in love with Richard Marlow you're so close to the brink that falling is a foregone conclusion. She took off her glasses and stared bleakly at the now-steamy walls.

Her whole professional life was rooted in practicalities. Every day she taught children to tackle problems realistically, to look ahead and consider the implications of their decisions and actions. Realistically, the implications of loving Richard were horrific. It wouldn't be just a private emotion between the two of them, the whole world would know about it. She couldn't hope to duck the frightening publicity that surrounded him. The Education Board might turn a blind eye to some of the 'alternative' life-styles of its teachers, but it would definitely balk at having a sex-symbol's mistress on the pay-roll, particularly if she had influence over a class of 'borderline delinquents'. Even if she loved Richard desperately she didn't know if she would sacrifice her career for him. It was a large part of her life, and turning her back on it would be like tearing herself in half. It obviously didn't occur to Richard that loving him would pose problems for her. And equally obviously he didn't equate love with a lasting relationship. He said he was 'in love' with her, therefore she was expected to fall into his bed, to move in with him, to accommodate herself completely to his alien life-style. They wouldn't be truly sharing their lives, because it would be Joanna making all the compromises—moral, emotional, physical. She would not only be sacrificing her career and reputation, but also all fond hopes of a quiet, loving, secure future. Joanna wasn't so naïve that she expected Richard to propose anything as outrageous as *marriage* but, if he had really loved her, wouldn't he have sensed all her doubts and hastened to reassure her that his flippant invitation meant fidelity, commitment? Perhaps an invitation to share living quarters was as close to commitment as he would ever get. Should she snatch at it, and be grateful for small mercies?

Traitorous thought! God, she didn't even dare let herself be *friends* with him; she didn't trust herself, the temptations would be too fierce.

So fierce that they haunted her sleep that night, and she

woke horrified by the insidious workings of her subconscious. In her dreams, they even had a *dog* to run with the little red-headed boys! Joanna cleaned her teeth viciously, deliberately leaving her glasses off so that she couldn't dwell on her morbid reflection. She couldn't look any worse than she felt, surely?

Having cleaned away the sweet taste of her dreams she went back to bed, determined that unrequited love (was love unrequited when the man you loved claimed to love you, but you didn't dare believe him?) was not going to deprive her of a much-deserved lie-in. She lay, brooding, and when the knock came at the door she hated herself for the way her heart began to pound.

'Go away or I'll call the police,' she yelled wildly. She might not be able to hide for ever, but she could have a damned good try.

'Er . . . ma'am?' came the cracked, uncertain reply. Such fractured tones could never have issued from Richard's golden throat. Cautiously, Joanna unlocked the door and peeped out of the crack at the teenage waiter balancing a covered tray in front of him.

'I didn't order room service,' Joanna frowned at him, opening the door wide once she had ascertained he was alone.

'Mr Marlow ordered it, ma'am,' said the young man. 'Shall I bring it in?'

Joanna was tempted to tell him exactly what he could do with Mr Marlow's breakfast order, but she was suddenly ravenous, and curious, too. Her eyes narrowed suspiciously. 'Is it for one or for two?

The waiter looked startled and speculative. 'For one, ma'am. Did you want to amend the order?'

Joanna blushed, furious with herself for putting ideas in his head. Now she couldn't send him away, he would think she had Richard hiding in the bathroom. 'You'd better bring it in.'

She got back into bed and allowed the waiter to place the tray across her knees and lift the cover. Her mouth watered

instantly at the delicious array: fresh juice, slices of melon
and iced out-of-season strawberries. Under a second cover,
keeping hot, were scrambled eggs with pale pink strips of
smoked salmon, melba toast and a fragrant, coffee-scented
cup of what the waiter told her was the chef's morning-after
special.

Morning after what? Joanna felt like asking, but she was
sure that the waiter had drawn his own conclusions.
Morning-after-finding-yourself-in-love-with-Mr Wrong,
Joanna decided as she tucked in, rationalising that it would
be a crime to waste such food ... it probably was budgeted-
in anyway: *breakfasts for director's current love interest(s):
amount of dollars.*

She was up and dressed, full stomach insisting on filling
her with unwelcome energy, when there was another
knock at her door.

'Who is it?' she called, trying for nonchalance over
outright panic.

'A reformed character,' came the ambiguous reply, but
the voice was unambiguous.

'You don't look it,' Joanna grinned, opening the door to
the haggard unshaven face, the slack jaw and pouched eyes
of Finn at his most disreputable.

'This is what abstinence does to me.' He returned her
grin. 'I have now been sober for at least ten minutes. Here,
I brought you a present.' He thrust the bottles of vodka
and whiskey into her hand and Joanna shuddered
involuntarily.

'"Farewell, thou Thing, time-past so knowne, so deare
to me, as blood to life and spirit".' Finn's mournful
declamation rang down the empty hallway.

'Huh?'

'Herrick's *Farewell to Sack*, but *my* sentiments.'

'Oh.' Joanna eyed him, debating the wisdom of con-
fession. 'I cheated, you know, I was feeding the pot plant.'

'Is that why I had to water it with aspirin this morning?'
Finn looked thoughtfully at her pale face. 'Cheats never
prosper you know, honey. Though to tell you the truth it

doesn't make a hell of a lot of difference. If I've got to give up it may as well be now. Did I do anything last night that I should apologise for, by the way?'

'Not to me, but you did take a swing at Richard.'

'And missed, he tells me. I wondered where the nice bruises came from when I woke up this morning . . . I didn't think they were from my usual slow glide into horizontal. Loren is going to brain me when she sees them, with these love scenes coming up, so I'm going to stagger out to buy her a sweetener; and send some flowers and something outrageously expensive to Bianca as a please-forgive-me-I-grovel victory present. Care to come along?'

'Just hang on, I'll get my jacket.' Joanna grabbed the opportunity to escape the hotel. It wasn't going to be easy to maintain her cool when she ran into Richard. Perhaps she could get some advice from Finn. He was Richard's friend, but she had no qualms about confiding in him. He had a healthy disrespect for his friend that might yield some magic formula. But, over coffee, after an extravagant raid on a jeweller's, Finn was sympathetic but not encouraging.

'Honey, Richard thrives on opposition, he's at his best with a challenge before him, whether it be a difficult scene or a difficult woman. To tell you the truth, I don't think I can recall a single woman he's set his sights on who hasn't succumbed in the end. He has a hell of a way with him.'

'Tell me something I don't know,' said Joanna, drooping over her cup, glad that she hadn't gone as far as confessing her love, only a violent and unwelcome attraction.

'You could do worse, darling,' Finn said gently, no fool in the ways of women himself. 'Much as I hate to blow his trumpet, since he does that all too well himself, Richard is a lovely man and he's made quite a few women desperately happy—oh, damn!' He looked disgusted with himself when she winced visibly. 'I've said the wrong thing, haven't I? Sorry, love. What I meant was that privately he's a very sensitive and caring man. He'd never deliberately hurt you, he has more emotional integrity in that direction than I ever did. And, as far as I know, he's never actually asked anyone to move in with him before. That must count for something. Maybe you should consider it.'

'I don't belong, Finn,' Joanna said with sad truth. 'I'm not cut out for his kind of life. I ... I want to be a good teacher, I want to combine that with a proper home and children ... the whole out-dated concept of "settling-down". I want contentment in my life, even if it means I don't get to hit the heights. Can you envisage Richard, even if he were madly in love with me, living an ordinary family life in the New Zealand suburbs? Of course not. What he wants, I can't give. What *I* need, *he* can't give.'

Finn's silence was tacit confirmation of all her own doubts and fears, and over the last, emotionally chaotic days of location filming, he proved himself a true friend by never volunteering an I-told-you-so when Richard responded to her attempts to keep their relationsip on a wholly professional level by breaking cover and carrying his ardent pursuit into the public arena. He languished beautifully, managing to look like a broken man with nothing to live for, even as he continued to direct his fierce energies into his film. Finn stuck effortlessly to diet sodas, spiced with daily phone calls to Europe; it was Joanna who felt like going out and getting drunk but, given her state of mind, she would probably hallucinate pink Marlows instead of nice, unthreatening pink elephants. She was furious, but unsurprised, when it turned out that Dean had opened book on the outcome of the romance, and the betting was heavily in Richard's favour.

'Ignore them, darling, you just go your own way,' Finn told her paternally, then spoiled it by adding slyly, 'I'm pretty well the only one betting on you, Joanna, so if you stick to your guns we stand to make a bundle. You can do it, kid. If I can give up the booze, you can give up Richard.'

It was a very apt analogy. It was like being an alcoholic, she discovered, craving for a look, a touch, a kiss and knowing that one would never be enough. One sweet taste and she would fall off the wagon with an almighty bang. If only there was a Lovers Anonymous she could join, for she was surrounded on all sides by addicts urging her to settle the bet in their favour.

Richard, with mischievous flamboyancy, had decided that the way to penetrate her hardened heart was through her stomach. He deluged her with choice favourites. Breakfast trays continued to arrive each morning, and each time that she returned to her room, some new basket of gastronomic goodies awaited her. Whatever she ordered for dinner, some additional exotic side dishes would turn up, dishes that would tempt the soul of a saint, let alone a self-confessed gourmand.

Even on location he didn't let up. Wherever they were—in the bush, on the beach, at David's cabin—each afternoon, as cast and crew gathered for their buffet lunch, a little van would arrive and two men in penguin suits would get out and home in on Joanna. White linen, starched napkins, red roses and food that brought tears to the eyes. No one would share with her, not even Becky—the sound of grinding axes audible from the sidelines. Just as disconcerting was the fact that Richard never tried to join her, he was too subtle for that. He left her in splendid isolation, content that with each mouthful she was ingesting the knowledge that he still wanted her, that he would have her. His confidence was shattering, his high spirits and good humour an insult. He didn't seem to care that time was running out, that soon she would be back home, out of his reach. It was just as Finn said—a challenge, a game. Love was a game.

The last straw was when Becky joined in—on Richard's side. On the second to last morning Joanna stared at her breakfast tray, torn between tears and laughter. Under the elegant silver cover was a neatly pre-packaged airline breakfast.

'I believe Mr Marlow had it specially sent down from the Air New Zealand kitchens in Auckland.' The young waiter grinned cheekily, delighted with his vicarious encounter with movie stars' antics.

'Why don't you give the poor guy a break, Aunty Jo?'

said Becky, collapsing on the bed as the waiter departed and helping herself to half a croissant and some marmalade.

'*Why?*' Joanna repeated incredulously, glaring at her happy, relaxed niece, wishing contrarily, that she had back the resentful, suspicious, infatuated girl of a few weeks ago.

'Yes, why?' Becky seemed to see no contradiction in her remark. 'I mean, you really give him a hard time. You're always so . . . schoolmarmish! I thought you liked him. You should give him a chance, he's only trying to show you what a nice guy he really is.'

'I know what he's trying to do, Becky, and nice isn't in it,' Joanna replied darkly.

'No, it'd be fantastic!' Becky munched on dreamily. 'If only he was a bit younger—about John's age. I mean, he's great and all that, and if he was plying *me* with hearts and flowers I'd probably be in bed with him in a flash; but I'd really rather have him as a director than as a lover. As a lover I'd only be famous by proxy. This way I get a spotlight all of my own.'

'*Becky!*' Joanna tried hard to sound horrified but her niece only grinned.

'Aw, come on, Aunty Jo, you can't expect me to pretend ignorance after going through those scenes I did with Finn. Isn't he a hunk? And he's older than Richard, even!'

'For God's sake, don't let your mother hear you say things like that,' Joanna shuddered, remembering that there was still that hill to climb. She still had to tell Ellen about the love scenes, but that was better done face to face she had judiciously decided. Actually, they had flowed smoothly, Becky soon overcoming her nervous giggles and even becoming bored with the intricacy of the procedure. Finn had been unembarrassed, relaxed, and joking, making a big production of covering up every time he came near Joanna, who conquered her blushes out of sheer self-defence. She hadn't been so successful when Richard chose to saunter over during a break and murmur teasingly,

'You like the way I handle a love scene?'

'I think Finn and Becky are doing marvellously,' she said, staring straight ahead, refusing to acknowledge the innuendo.

'You and I would be even more marvellous together.' His voice sank into a sexy purr. 'Only with us there'd be no holds barred: we'd both be naked . . . there'd be lights but no cameras, no audience. Just our own, very personal, private love scene . . . and if you wanted to direct it, darling, it would be a pleasure to work under you.'

She had gone bright red and he had laughed and ruffled her hair, and everyone had looked disgustingly expectant. It had ruined the day for her. From then on she couldn't rid herself of the picture he had projected on her mind, and she found herself projecting a few ideas of her own that were equally disturbing. Three more days . . . she clung to the lifeline . . . three more days. If she could hold on to her sanity for three more days she would be all right. Alcoholics were never truly cured, but abstinence was made easier by the absence of temptation!

CHAPTER NINE

'This is *au revoir*, you know, Joanna. Not goodbye.'

Joanna stared stonily into Richard Marlow's beguiling eyes, unbeguiled. Now she knew why he had insisted on driving them out to the airport. Since she had refused him a private farewell he was going to make her give him a public one. That was why he had encouraged the fans to follow them through the terminal to the check-in desk, and introduced Becky as the star of his new film. She was signing autographs now, delighted by the attention he had directed her way.

'Ellen will be coming with Becky to the studio for the rest of her scenes,' Joanna said coldly. 'My association with you ends right here.'

'Our professional association, yes,' he agreed, with twinkling eyes. 'But our *personal* association has only just begun.'

Joanna snorted. 'Try that line on your blonde floozie, she might believe it.'

'I am. You're my blonde floozie,' he grinned, with a hint of puzzlement.

Joanna opened her mouth for a sizzling retort when she heard someone in the crowd of avid listeners pipe up, 'Is she in the movie, too? Who is she?'

'——Dunno——' somebody else answered, and Joanna gave an inward shudder, hoping it would stay that way. She looked around, desperate for escape, and surprisingly, it was Richard who provided it. He took her by the hand and stalked over to the relative privacy of the departure gate, exercising the privilege of fame on the flight attendant checking tickets at the door, leaving Becky still eagerly entertaining the fans.

'Surely you didn't expect it to be over just because filming was over?' Richard said with tender sternness when they were out in the crisp, clear air but still in full view of the terminal. 'Darling! No wonder you've been so standoffish. I thought you realised. Of *course* it's not going to end. I love you——' his mouth curved, 'and I've invested far too much time and energy, not to mention food, in you to let you walk out of my life now ...'

'I hardly think you're going to miss me, Richard,' Joanna said sarcastically, shivering as the wind swept up under her padded jacket. 'No doubt you'll find someone else to fill the minuscule gap I leave in your busy life.'

'There is no one else,' he said, with a devout simplicity that made her blister.

'Not even the blonde I saw you falling all over last night in that bar?'

He looked astonished, then amused. 'Julia? You mean *Julia?*' He laughed. 'You can't be jealous of *Julia*! I didn't see you there, why didn't you come over and say hello?'

'And interrupt your contemplation of her navel?' she

said frigidly. She had sent his breakfast offering back this morning, unable to stomach a single morsel of his hypocrisy. She had supped bitter black coffee in the restaurant instead, and tried to blame her queasiness on lack of food.

She had thought it odd at the time that Richard should only make a brief appearance at the crew's location wrap-up party and then disappear. Later, when a cold-stricken Kelly offered to go back to the hotel with Becky, Joanna had discovered the reason for Richard's defection. The party degenerated very quickly into a bar-crawl with the only two wowsers, Joanna and Finn, supervising the rest of the boisterous company. They ended up in a very crowded, smoky bar near the hotel, and who should Joanna spy tucked away in the darkest corner but Richard and a strange blonde.

Fortunately for her pride, no one else noticed him, and Richard certainly wasn't seeing anything but the blonde. She was tiny, but shaped like a dream and showing a great deal of what she had in a low-cut dress. She had the kind of curls that Shirley Temple would have envied and to Joanna she looked exactly like a little doll—an adult, inflatable doll, she decided cattily.

Unable to prevent herself, Joanna skulked through the crush for a better look, just to make sure she wasn't mistaken. Luckily, they were in the general direction of the powder-room, which would provide her with the perfect excuse if Richard did happen to lift his eyes from that enviable cleavage.

The blonde had blue eyes that were sparkling and full of fun. The two of them, laughing over drinks, looked painfully like kindred spirits. Joanna knew, with an instinctive dread, that this was the *she* that he had talked so delightedly about on the phone. No wonder he had been so keen!

As Joanna hesitated behind a clump of potted plastic plants wondering whether to go on into the powder-room and indulge in more pointless tears, or to go back to the bar and order a triple vodka, she caught a drift of conversation that sent her straight to the bottle.

'. . . I've been dying to tell all and sundry,' the woman was saying with a gusty sigh,' but I suppose our families would be miffed if they weren't the first to know. And none of your silly tricks, Richard, leave the announcement to me. I mean, I love you—practical jokes and all—but even I can take only so much . . .'

'A hell of a lot, actually, darling, judging by the size of my——'

'Richard!' the loving threat cut off Richard's laughing leer and Joanna's teeth grated with the effort of remaining silent. She lingered an instant longer to complete her disillusionment.

'. . . And I love you, too, darling,' said Richard, his voice enriched with warmth. 'Of course I won't steal your thunder. I only wish . . . oh, damn . . . I had such plans for us when Mama rang to tell me you were coming, but there've been complications . . .'

Namely, me, thought Joanna wretchedly as she fled. Two-timing louse! Even when he knew his lover's arrival was imminent he hadn't stopped trying to seduce Joanna. The man was not only a compulsive liar, he was a compulsive lover!

'Joanna,' the two-faced swine was saying now. 'I admit that there are a lot of things I find fascinating about women, but navels aren't one of them . . . except for yours, of course. I would have loved you two to meet, I want to show off the woman I love——'

'I'm not surprised, she's very pretty,' said Joanna, icily.

'Not *her*, *you*,' he said in exasperation. 'Naturally I love Julia, we go way back——' he was even admitting it!

'——but I love a lot of people in different ways——'

'So I've noticed,' Joanna snapped.

'Will you shut up and listen,' he ordered confidently. 'You're going to laugh when you hear this——' Joanna severely doubted it. 'I'll admit that once, in the greenness of youth, I *did* think I was in love with Julia, but it didn't take

me very long to realise that it wasn't love in the classical
sense of the word——'.

'In the classical sense of the word, Richard, you're fickle!'
Joanna hissed at him. 'The world must be littered with
women that you thought you were in love with, *at the time*.
How exhausting it must be, emotionally, to have to fall *in
love* every time you want to satisfy a physical urge. How
awkward that Julia's time should come round again before
mine is quite expired——'

'Joanna, for God's sake!' He wasn't so confident now she
had taken his measure. 'This is all a misunderstanding. You
can't leave like this——'

Watch me! her expression said, and he caught her
shoulder and accused in a scornful growl, 'I suppose you're
going to go running back to that freckled full-back of yours
just because he seems nice and safe. He's all wrong for you,
Joanna, can't you see that? Can't you see what you're
throwing away here . . .?'

She looked him up and down in a way that made his jaw
tighten. 'Yes. That's why I'm throwing it away. Now let me
go. Becky and I have a plane to catch.'

'Joanna——' he began with grim impatience; then his
eyes drifted over the top of her head and narrowed. A
strange calculating gleam kindled in their depths. Joanna
tried to turn around and see what had caught his attention,
but he bent and spoke so close to her spectacles that they
fogged up and she could see nothing.

'All right, silly blind owl. If that's the way you want to
play it . . .'

And while she was still befogged he swept her into his
arms and kissed her, a long impassioned embrace worthy of
the best swashbuckling tradition. She was still gasping,
flushed and flustered, when he called Becky and hustled
them across the tarmac.

Home welcomed her, cosily familiar, but unfortunately not
a haven of peaceful obscurity. The very day of her arrival
there was Ellen . . .

Her sister took the news of Becky's loves scenes with suspicious calm. Joanna wished that she could cut and run while the going was good, but she had promised Becky that she would broach the subject of her future as soon as possible. Sure enough, a single sentence sent Ellen's beautifully coiffured head through the ceiling.

'What do you mean, you think that Becky ought to go to *drama* school?' she abandoned her thin-lipped silence to shriek. 'She's going to University for her science degree, you know that! We planned it before she ever went for that blessed audition. You were *supposed* to keep Becky's feet on the ground, not encourage her adolescent whims. How you can even suggest it, I don't know, *you* know the value of a good education.' Suspicion made her glassy-eyed. 'Or is this your way of telling me that the wretched girl is going to fail bursary after all——'

'Of course she'll pass, she's worked harder than any of us expected her to; partly, I think, to show you that she *can*,' Joanna interrupted the tirade. 'But this is more than a whim. She has talent and she's prepared to work at it far more ambitiously then she'll ever work at chemistry or physics. I'm not saying you should make a decision now, but it wouldn't hurt to leave it until the end of the year, until she's passed her exams and you've seen the film for yourself. She can always go to University, but the kind of chances that are going to come her way when the film is released only come once in a lifetime. And don't forget, Ellen, that it won't be long before she won't *have* to ask for your permission, or your blessing, on her career. If you deny her your trust and confidence now you might lose her altogether . . .'

When she finally managed to extricate herself from the argument, she departed with a whispered injunction to an anxious Becky to lay off for a while. Ellen wasn't stupid, just stubborn, and time might eventually succeed where direct pressure failed. Becky wasn't the same girl who had left home nearly a month ago, there was a sense of purpose about her that her mother would soon recognise for herself.

Hard on the heels of one confrontation came another. Duncan was every bit as hurt and bewildered as she had feared he would be, when she told him that her time away had made her see she was drifting into a relationship that she didn't really want. Naturally, he asked if there was another man and Joanna felt horribly guilty denying it, but she had her pride. She knew all too well what a fool she had been, she didn't need to have anyone else point it out to her. Besides, there wasn't another man, not any more . . .

. . . Except in her heart. Richard had made a pretty thorough job of infiltrating himself there. Even after only a few days she missed his constant, enlivening, aggravating presence, his teasing eyes and his flirting smile. Her feelings formed a small, hard knot inside her that drew ever tighter until she felt as if it was the only thing holding her together.

What she was trying so hard to forget, everyone else was eager for her to remember. If Richard himself had bribed her classes they couldn't have worked any harder to get her to relive her experiences of the past few weeks in excruciating detail. For once they were actually insatiable for knowledge, and Joanna found herself desperately pining for the old days when the invitation: 'Any questions?' invariably provoked a flurry of loud yawns in response.

The days passed with tiresome slowness, the hectic business of living merely emphasising the inner emptiness. For the first time in her professional life, Joanna felt alienated from the hopes and aspirations of her pupils and had to struggle not to resent their cheerful, adolescent selfishness.

Richard haunted her, not only at school, but at home as well. Television New Zealand were running a retrospective of his films and each evening Joanna was riveted unwillingly to the screen, watching the object of her obsession risk his life every ten minutes, in between seducing gorgeous, gullible women who seemed to fall into his bed as soon as look at him. It might only be 'simulated' in Richard's words but it was painfully well acted. Joanna closed her eyes during those sequences, then cheated through squinted lids. At least *they* got to share his bed, even if it meant getting bumped off by the villain five minutes later, she thought sourly. Joanna hadn't permitted herself the luxury of even *that* risk, and she was beginning to feel that particular act of self-denial was going to prove the supremely masochistic experience of her life. The first great love affair of her life, and what did she have to show for it? Nothing. She still didn't know what it felt like to share the fullness of love with another human being. Now it would be another man, not Richard, to whom she gave the gift of her innocence, and she had the awful feeling that the prize would be going to a runner-up.

The weekend held no joy. Saturday was spent doing chores, and on Sunday morning she lay in bed wondering if she dare ring up Duncan and suggest their usual Sunday jaunt. No, that wouldn't be fair on him. She would clean the oven instead. She was still trying to get enthused about the idea when the telephone dragged her out of her gloomy bed.

'Joanna, how *could* you? A fine chaperon *you* turned out to be! No wonder you're suddenly all-fired keen on Becky becoming an actress! Just how long were you going to keep it a secret? And encouraging Becky to keep secrets too, from her own *mother*! How that man has been able to look me in the eye all week *I* don't know—he hasn't even *mentioned* you, and all the time you've been sneaking around ...! You could at least have *warned* me, instead of leaving me to read about it in the paper ... the *Sunday* paper of all things! I'm very, *very* disappointed in you, Joanna——'

'Ellen——'

'*No*. I'm just too upset to even *talk* about it. I'll see *you* later!'

'Ellen! Ellen?' Joanna shook the dead receiver as if her sister might fall out of it. Then she flew down to her letter-box, not even stopping to put on a robe.

They were on page three, where the half-naked woman usually was. MARLOW MARRIAGE MYSTERY, screamed the headline, bannering across four photographs of Richard and an easily identifiable Joanna in an increasingly passionate clinch.

'Who is the mystery woman in actor/director Richard Marlow's life?' the caption ran tantalisingly. 'Marlow, who habitually conducts his love-life in a blaze of publicity, has been unusually coy about the woman he was caught kissing at New Plymouth airport this week. Can it be because this time it's serious for the one-time Academy Award winner and sex symbol? Sources tell us that Marlow has finally got over his bust-up with Bianca James and mended fences with her husband, former best friend Finn Tracey, in time to invite them to the wedding. Yes, fans, it seems that Marlow is finally tying the knot ... but with whom? The first person to call this newspaper with the mystery fiancée's identity will win a free pass to the première of Marlow's new movie, due out early in the New Year ...'

There was more about the film, but Joanna's attention was drawn back to the betraying photographs. Who had taken them? A fan? Oh, damn Richard for encouraging all that attention! And who were these fictitious 'sources' who were hinting marriage? Probably a case of the reporter interviewing his typewriter, she decided cynically, hence his 'unusually coy' remark about Richard. If he had *really* spoken to Richard he would have received a flat denial, she was sure, particularly in view of the 'announcement' that he and his ever-loving Julia intended to make soon. Would that be marriage? Or something more flexible ...? What should she do? Joanna asked herself, trying to eclipse the bitter speculation with the desire for action. Ring up and complain? But that might mean revealing her identity.

Not that it appeared to be very secret. By mid-morning Joanna was contemplating putting her head in the oven, but not to clean it! There were calls of astonishment, curiosity and congratulations from acquaintances and friends, and friends-of-friends, even the man from the corner dairy. People believed what they wanted to believe, she discovered in frustration, and everyone wanted to believe that someone thay knew was involved in a torrid romance with a superstar. The hardest to take were the ones from her new-found film friends, delighted to a man and complaining with good-natured wrath that Finn had unfairly scooped the betting pool. Dean declared that to compensate he was starting one up on the sex of their first child, and merely laughed when she said the story was complete rubbish.

'That's not what Richard says,' he told her before he hung up. 'He's put fifty bucks on male twins. See you at the wedding, honey ...'

As soon as she replaced the receiver it rang again and she contemplated throwing it through the window. So Richard thought it was funny, did he? That was par for the course. Meanwhile, she had to put up with this!

'What?' she snarled into the mouthpiece, intending to be short, sharp and sour, whoever it was.

'Have you seen the newspapers?'

Richard. Her intention crumbled into dust. 'I have seen *a* newspaper, Richard, that was enough.'

'Have you spoken to anyone from the Press?'

Defensively, she rushed into the breach. 'Of course I haven't. I didn't have anything to do with the story. I didn't even know anyone was taking pictures. I have no idea who would say such things——'

'Me.'

'You?' Joanna sat down with a thump on the cold kitchen floor.

'I gave them the story.'

'*You?*' A small, fierce flame began to flicker in the hollow of her heart. 'You? But ... why? *Why?*' The receiver slipped in her hands so she almost missed his reply.

'Publicity.'

'Publicity? *Publicity!*' The flame was consumed by a more intense blaze.

'I knew the photographer was there when I kissed you, but there was no guarantee they'd run the picture unless

there was a juicy caption to run with it. You see, darling, I
wanted to——'

She didn't hear what he wanted to do. She slammed the
telephone down and ran out of the house. She had fallen in
love with a monster! He had used her simply for the sake of
some cheap, sensationalist publicity for his film!

Just how sensationalist was proven over the next few
days. Her categorical denials were greeted with healthy
scepticism by the reporters and photographers who
converged on school and apartment, thanks to 'super-grass'
Teresa. Carson mania gripped the school. Girls began to
sport 'Carson cuts' and unglassed spectacles and, when
Joanna actually discovered a budding entrepreneur in her
home room selling forgeries of her signature and people
sneaking *in* to her English grammar classes, she finally
admitted to Duncan that things were out of hand.

'The only way you're going to get rid of the Press and
cool things down is to give them what they want: an
interesting story,' he said, somewhat unsympathetically.
She couldn't blame him for his coolness, she had lied to him
and now he knew it, although he was friend enough to
believe her when she confessed the truth—that she *was* in
love with Richard but they had never been lovers, and now
never would be.

'But what'll I say?' she asked helplessly. 'That we're just
good friends? Who's going to believe that when even my
own sister won't!' That was the single plus in the situation.
Ellen had refused to speak to her for three days. Three
whole days without Ellen's nagging accusations!

'You'll think of something,' Duncan said gruffly. 'I'll
support you with the Education Board, but I can't get
unofficially involved without compromising that support.
They're sending an inspector out next week, so let's hope
that it's all blown over by then.'

An inspector! The thought panicked Joanna into rash
action. Why should she have to pay for Richard's perfidy?
He was making no attempt at all to defuse the rumours,
merely issuing reporters with smug smiles which belied his

uncharacteristic 'no comments'. It wasn't just the publicity for his film, she thought savagely, he was also using the fuss to conceal his *real* affair. He was using Joanna to protect Julia until they were ready to go public. Well, Joanna wasn't going to play the fall guy. She would shape her own destiny, especially if it meant putting a kink in Richard's! By now, everyone assumed they were lovers, so there was only one way she could think of to restore a whiff of respectability to the situation and thus cover herself with the Education Board ...

Joanna called a press conference to announce the termination of her secret engagement to Richard Marlow.

She was rather horrified at the ease and pleasure with which she creatively embroidered the truth for the eagerly assembled scribes. She put on a sadder-but-wiser face and confessed that it was Richard's peripatetic life—and love—style that had caused the irreconcilable rift. She regretted the malicious impulse to add the 'love' when the remark prompted some very specific questions.

'——Does that mean there's another woman——?'
'——Who is she——?'
'——Is it your niece, Becky Turner——?'

Oh God, she didn't want to lose Ellen's goodwill permanently! Joanna cast around for the proper bait, but at the last minute she couldn't utter the betrayal. If Julia could make Richard happy, even briefly, so be it. Let them have their precious privacy.

'I think he's been seeing a skier.' She assumed a great reluctance and allowed the meagre details to be dragged from her. 'I'm not sure what her name is, Gerda something, I think. She's some kind of European ski champion who's here recovering from an injury. That's all I know, truly,' she raised her voice over the clamour. 'If you want to know any more you'll have to talk to Richard ...' She wasn't going to let him get off entirely scot-free.

She closed the door on the last clicking camera with a grin of relief. There was a certain satisfaction in knowing that she had handled herself like a pro. Not that there would be any need, in her placid future—placid, she assured herself, *not* boring—to use such knowledge.

Still, she almost enjoyed reading the ensuing stories, content to see herself demoted from 'jilted bride' to 'dumped fiancée' to a quite respectable 'former fiancée'. She hid the cuttings in the back of a drawer. Perhaps one day she might feel strong enough to take them out and laugh over them, laugh over the whole miserable affair . . .

'Hello, Joanna! We haven't met, but I feel I know you well already . . .'

Joanna wilted. Another fan. The Press might be off baying around the country's ski-fields, but fans were of a hardier breed. The voice on the telephone sounded rather mature, but she had discovered in the past week that Richard's fan club was composed of all sorts and all ages, and they had elected *her* temporary information officer.

'I'm sorry, I'm rather busy right now——' Heavens, she was even beginning to sound like Richard. So did the woman at the other end, come to that. Perhaps it was an insidious form of flattery.

'I know, I know . . . Richard does tend to have that kind of influence on one's life, but don't worry I won't keep you, I'm just ringing up to say a brief hello. I would have called sooner, but Michael and I have been away and absolutely snowed *under* with work, but we're back now and looking forward to meeting you . . .'

'M . . . Mrs *Marlow*?' croaked Joanna, suddenly realising *why* the woman sounded so much like Richard.

'Connie. I'm Connie to the family and I'm delighted that you're going to be one of us . . . Richard has told me *so* much about you . . . Why don't we get together one day for lunch and swap horror stories about him? Or is lunch difficult, with your job? Dinner, then . . . you can meet Charley then, too—he's still living at home. And there's Hugh and his wife . . . or perhaps it might be better if you met us in ones and twos, we do rather overwhelm people *en masse*, though

if you can put up with Richard you can probably cope with
anything ...'

'Mrs Marlow—Connie——' Joanna broke in hurriedly,
'Richard and I aren't ... er ... have you read the papers?'

'Mmmm? Oh, yes ... very clever of you, my dear. Gerda
has helped us once or twice in the past when one of us wants
to shake off the Press, she's practically a family institution
by now!' A laugh so unnervingly like Richard's than
Joanna felt her knees weaken. 'Richard was very pleased at
the way you pulled it off. Thank goodness he's fallen for a
woman of intelligence and not one of those horrendously
silly females who've tried to fling themselves at him in the
past. Richard needs someone he can *respect*. He's told me
about your reservations, but I can assure you, Joanna, that
he's very much in love ...'

Yes, but who with? thought Joanna, as she shakily put
the phone down after much more in the same warm and
informative vein. She hadn't found the courage to puncture
the woman's obvious pleasure. Was Julia from the ranks of
the 'horrendously silly'? Was that why Richard had been
generating his smoke-screen of lies? But it was his mother
who had rung him in New Plymouth to tell him of Julia's
visit. Would she have done that if she didn't approve of
their alliance? Joanna began to simmer with frustrated
indignation. Richard had no right to involve her in his
family problems! How embarrassing it was going to be for
his mother when she discovered that she had welcomed the
wrong woman into the Marlow clan! She would probably
want to ring back and apologise, and Joanna would die a
thousand humiliating deaths ...

She rang the studio, intending to leave a very succinct,
threatening message for Richard but unfortunately, as soon
as the cheerful telephonist heard Joanna's name, she put her
straight through to his extension.

'Hello, Joanna,' he greeted her, with enraging smugness.
'What can I do for you?'

'This has gone far enough, Richard——'

'I agree. You really must stop flaunting yourself before

the world's Press darling. All those terrible lies! I was quite shocked when I read them——'

'*Richard!*' Her vocal chords protested the yell. 'I've just had a call from your mother——'

'Oh, good. She said she was going to ring. Did she suggest dinner?'

'——Richard, you've got to tell her the truth——'

'But I did. I told her I loved you and wanted to marry you and live happily ever after. She was thrilled.' He chuckled.

'Well *I'm* not!' She was shattered by the casual way he made a joke of her deepest, most secret desires. 'And if you don't stop involving me in your stupid schemes I'll ... I'll ...'

'... Feed more lies to the Press?'

'If that's what it takes!'

'Brave little owl.' His voice suddenly dropped its banter and became low and disturbingly intense. 'Didn't I tell you, that day I tried to teach you to ski, that you could learn to live with the pressures of my life? You refused to believe it then, but I think you've proved otherwise since, haven't you? That's why I planted that story, darling, to show you that, while publicity is a nuisance, it's not a real threat to our private happiness ... it can even be fun sometimes!

'So what do you say, shall we get married and confound the journalists with a new twist? If you're still doubtful, look at it this way: you've weathered all the hassles of being engaged to me already, so you're over the worst. You may as well marry me and have done with it!'

For a micro-second Joanna was speechless. He had turned her life into a three-ring circus just to prove a *point*? Just to get his own way? And he was asking, no *assuming*, that she'd leap at the chance of marrying him even though she knew he was in love with another woman ...!

'Go to hell, Richard Marlow!' she screamed down the line. 'I wouldn't marry you if it meant the extinction of the species. And I never, ever *ever* want to see or hear from you *ever again*!'

CHAPTER TEN

'Oh, Miss Carson, isn't this just so incredibly *choice*!'

'Incredibly,' said Joanna grimly, longing to brain the pretty dark-haired girl chattering excitedly beside her. The last thing she needed at the moment was Teresa rabbiting on about how awesome and choice life was. Life was not.

Joanna groaned silently to herself. Anyone else would have had the decency, the dignity, to slink miserably away after a brutal rejection, but not Richard. Oh no! The very next day he had been on the telephone to Duncan, setting up this studio tour for her class. The *nerve*! And Duncan had actually swallowed the bait hook, line and sinker, and told Joanna it was her duty to put personal considerations aside for the good of the school.

Men were total idiots! Look at the way her notorious delinquents were hanging on Richard's every word as they trailed him around the film studio facilities ... the same raucous young toughs who'd spent the bus trip across town making obscene gestures out of the back window to total strangers! As for the girls ... God knows what had possessed Duncan to let them come in mufti, perhaps he didn't want to risk their disgracing the school uniform. The giggles and whispers and slyly bold questions to Richard were almost drowned out by the clatter of enough junk jewellery to sink the Titanic.

Though she had refused to look at him directly, she knew that Richard was looking his usual gorgeous self in stone-washed denims and a loose white silk shirt. Joanna, in a defiantly plain dress none the less found she was attracting as much attention in the busy studio as Richard. She returned the waves and greetings weakly. The reverberations of her little fling with the Press were still being felt in some quarters. She wondered if Dean was still making book on the future little Marlows—that might explain all the nods and winks ...

Her class were revelling in the reflected glory of her pseudo-celebrity status. As usual, Richard had judged his audience perfectly. When he had dropped his bombshell suggestion that he take the whole lot of them out to lunch, they had made it very, very clear that they would never forgive the hitherto favoured Miss Carson if she did them out of this one. Knowing well just how relentlessly unforgiving C5 could be—the same reason she hadn't dared refuse the offer of a tour—she acquiesced with a killing look at Richard.

He countered her last-ditch objection with an unarguable—'I can afford it. I'm rich. And it comes under *publicity* and entertainment ... it's tax deductible.'

His deliberate use of the hated word so infuriated Joanna that she marched her motley crew to the restaurant around the corner from the warehouse-like studio building with drill-sergeant discipline, only balking when they got inside the monogrammed glass doors and the red mist cleared enough from her eyes that she could see where they were.

'Richard, we can't eat *here*,' she hissed, forgetting that she had promised herself she wouldn't address another word to him. 'When you said a restaurant I thought you meant MacDonalds ... or a family-type place.'

'What's the matter? Don't you think the kids can handle a little high-class eating?'

Twenty-four pairs of eyes scorched Joanna's face. She saved face with a gritty warning. 'It'll cost a fortune.'

'It'll be worth it,' Richard murmured with a bland crypticism that rang alarm bells the size of Notre-Dame's. 'Hello, Michael, are our tables ready?'

Joanna digested the fact that he had pre-booked, and that the stiff, dark-suited Michael didn't flicker an eyelash at the sight of the crowd of teenagers noisily appreciating the décor. Her misgivings increased as they were shown to a group of tables in the centre of the room, by-passing the mostly middle-aged, business-suited men and snappily-dressed women who made up the rest of the clientele.

'Hey, wow, look at all that silver——' She heard the hoarse whisper of the entrepreneur who had cleaned-up selling her signatures, and snapped around with grim command:

'*No* souveniring, Haskins!' She prolonged the gimlet stare just long enough to miss out on having a say in the seating arrangements.

'You and I will sit over here.' Richard pointed to a table for four as the class seated themselves in a rush, leaving Joanna standing like the odd one out in musical chairs.

'I think I ought to sit at one of the big tables, to keep an eye on things . . .'

'Michael will do that, won't you, Michael? He has eight kids himself and grew up on the streets of Naples. You can't get better qualified than that. Sit down, Joanna, you're attracting attention.'

She did, hurriedly, as he knew she would, casting furtive looks around her. Teresa, never one to let an opportunity slide, leapt to her feet.

'I'll sit at your table, Miss Carson——'

'You stay right where you are, darling,' Richard gave her a force-ten smile that fused her to the spot. 'Just keep your Cupid's bow handy; Miss Carson and I may need it.'

Teresa giggled, while Joanna wistfully eyed the knife at her left hand. 'I already used it. I was the one who got you two together. Don't you remember her asking you for an autograph for Teresa that day you visited our school?'

Joanna contemplated turning the knife on herself as she heard Richard say, 'I remember a girl with a hockey stick . . .'

'That was Miss Carson, dressed up!' Teresa supplied gleefully. 'Didn't you know?'

Richard began to laugh, a rich, mellow laugh that turned the heads that weren't already turned. Joanna cringed, refusing to look at him as he took his seat opposite her, still laughing, lazily adjusting his legs under the table so that they brushed against her primly tucked ones. 'You tantalising little devil,' he chuckled as she buried herself behind the large, gilt menu. 'So that's how we met! No wonder I couldn't remember. Actually you reminded me of a bird then, too, only it was a crow not an owl ...'

It gave Joanna a pretty sense of revenge to choose the most expensive dish on the menu for her order, but Richard topped her by ordering the same for himself.

'Relax, Joanna,' he said as she listened anxiously to the loud vacillations going on behind her, and wished that she had sat facing her pupils. 'Let them enjoy themselves, they'll rise to the occasion. I didn't bring you here to embarrass you——'

'Why *did* you bring me?'

He leaned his chin on bridged hands, the dark flecks showing vividly in the green eyes as he spoke. 'Neutral ground. I get the feeling you'd slam the door on me if I turned up at your flat, and you don't speak to me on the telephone——'

'You had no right to say those things about me to your mother,' she interrrupted him, in a low, fierce voice.

'I don't see why I should keep it a secret, I'm not ashamed of loving you. Whether you love me in return or not is irrelevant, I shall still love *you*. OK, so it was impulsive and high-handed of me to set the Press on you, but I was getting desperate and I honestly thought that a practical experiment was the only way I was going to convince you to give me a chance. As for my proposal——'

'That wasn't a proposal, that was an insult——'

'I *had* meant to do it with soft lights and music over an intimate dinner, but my impatience got the better of me. I do want to marry you, Joanna Carson, I swear——'

'Because you can't have me any other way?' she asked bitterly.

He looked astonished, then amused. 'Joanna, darling ...' he drawled. 'I think we both know that if I really tried I could have you any way I wanted you ...'

He watched with satisfaction the evasive flutter of her

big brown eyes, the faint flush skimming under the opaque skin. Ah yes, he wasn't wrong about *that* at least, his little owl still wanted him quite as fiercely as he wanted her. Richard felt the slow, slumberous stir of his body. His need was so great that he would trap her with her own desires if necessary, and later try his damnedest to make her want to stay of her own free will. But, God, she *had* to love him, the belief was what kept him sane. He must make her admit her feelings, admit that her distrust of him stemmed not so much from his failings as from her own insecurities. In a way it was the mental equivalent of her needless inferiority complex about her lovely little body. All his clever plans had so far only succeeded in making her dig her stubborn heels in; if today's didn't work he would just have to try and wipe the slate clean and start all over again, the hard way, her way ... slow and steady. He groaned softly.

'... Do you put all your lovers to the rack like this? I ache all over just thinking about how it would be for us ...'

'I don't have lovers,' Joanna snapped, shattered by the dreamily sensual curve of his mouth, the sea-green depths of his eyes as they loved her as his body would like to do.

'What, none?' An interrogative eyebrow teased her.

'Never!'

He choked on his glass of iced water and looked at her in a way that made her want to laugh, or cry, or hit him—or do all three at once. Was he looking for defects?

'Are you serious?' he asked hoarsely.

Furious at betraying herself but refusing to back down, Joanna pinched her mouth into disapproval. 'Not everyone treats sex with the casual flippancy that you do.'

'You're a virgin? My owl is still a fledgling?' Did he want it in writing, for goodness sake?

'Yes, I'm a virgin ... no thanks to you,' she said with frigid clarity.

He coughed again and looked down at his plate. 'Er ... Joanna, I think the waiter wants to ...'

Joanna's head whipped around to see the scarcely concealed grin of the waiter standing beside their table with two steaming plates in his hands. She also saw the frankly assessing stare of the businessman at the next table and the smirk of his companion. With a cry of embarrassment and rage she buried her face in her linen napkin, whence not even the mouth-watering fragrance of lobster in Sauce Américaine could lure her.

Richard, several delicious comments hovering on the tip of his tongue, wisely controlled himself and began to eat, contemplating yet another hideous example of his hypocrisy. He was delighted. A virgin! What an exquisite experience it would be to teach his fledgling to fly. Providing, he thought, as he surveyed the top of the silky cropped head, he didn't get pecked to death in the process.

'Hello, you two! That looks good. I'm famished. Can I have a seat?'

Joanna looked up at the sound of the cheerful voice. *Julia* stood there, exactly where the grinning waiter had been, a look of such blooming sweetness on her face that Joanna almost liked her on the spot. She restrained herself just in time. It was the last straw.

'Certainly. Here, take mine.' Forgetting her class, happily stuffing themselves with exotica behind her, Joanna steamed out of the restaurant, straight into the side of a building.

The building moved, steadying her with a large hand. 'Sorry. Are you all right?'

Joanna cranked her neck back and straightened her glasses. He was big. 'Sorry, my fault——' she muttered, and then she saw what he was holding in his other hand. A small baby in a blue stretch-and-grow suit to match his bright blue eyes, thumb in mouth.

'I know, we look ridiculous together don't we?' the giant rumbled, reading her mind, the wintry grey eyes thawing into a gentle smile. Joanna saw the resemblance immediately. The baby's jaw was tiny, but definitely very square. The hair was blond as opposed to the man's pure grey, but both crops were thick and straight. 'But he was born prematurely and he hasn't quite caught up with his peers yet. I'm told he'll probably be my size one day. This is Ben.'

'Hello, Ben,' said Joanna obediently, feeling her numb brain suddenly mesh again. She was twenty-four people short.

'Has my wife arrived yet?' the big man asked her as he held open the glass door for her re-entry. 'She was catering a champagne breakfast in town this morning for one of her regular clients and I was left literally holding the baby.'

'Your wife?' Joanna repeated blankly, wondering who he was mistaking her for.

'Oh, I'm sorry, Joanna, I suppose I assumed that because I recognised you, you'd automatically know me. I'm Hugh Walton, Richard's brother—adopted brother if you're wondering about the name and lack of resemblance. Julia is my wife.'

'Julia? Your *wife*?' Joanna squeaked dizzily. 'But . . . I thought . . . she and Richard . . .'

Grey eyebrows rose and he looked mildly amused. 'So did Richard at one time. Thankfully, Julia is a woman of discernment and taste, and realised that it was I, not Richard, who really needed her—and fell in love accordingly. He was my best man and, to show me all was forgiven, he extracted all my money and credit cards from my wallet just before we left on honeymoon and replaced them with confetti.'

'What did you do?' Joanna asked, fascinated by his deadpan expression.

'Fortunately, I discovered the joke before we got to the airport. We made a brief detour to Richard's flat.' He paused, and Joanna discovered this big, quiet-voiced man had his own sense of theatre. 'We pawned his Oscar.'

Joanna began to laugh.

'I told you you'd laugh but you wouldn't listen,' Richard said smugly, swiftly re-seating her and greeting his elder brother and nephew. Joanna's laugh turned into a scowl and Julia Walton rushed into the breach.

'I don't blame you for not listening to him, he manages to make the simplest of explanations complicated.' Joanna couldn't help returning the sympathetic grin. 'He should have told you that I was coming down for my chef's seminar, not tried to spring one of his famous surprises.' She passed Richard's bread roll across the table and Hugh used it to mute his son's babble. 'Honestly, Richard, you'd think that you got enough of plotting and scene-setting at work!'

'*You* can talk,' he retorted. 'What about this grand plan of yours for a mass family gathering to announce that you're pregnant again?'

Pregnant? Joanna suddenly remembered the conversation she had overheard in the bar and blushed at the conclusions she had leapt to. 'The size of my . . .' *brother*!

'Embarrassed, darling?' Richard asked wickedly when he noticed her blush. 'She's already announced it to the restaurant at large, so I may as well tell you two: Joanna is still a virgin, chaste and shy.'

'I'll *kill* you!' she ground out, not knowing where to look.

'"Alas, poor Romeo, he is already dead! Stabbed by a white wench's black eye; shot through the ear with a love song",' Hugh murmured softly, and astonishment penetrated Joanna's embarrassment. It was the sort of thing she would expect Richard to say, not this very solid-looking man in his conservative suit and rather grave expression.

'He looks like a stuffy bear, but actually he has the heart and soul of a poet,' Julia confirmed, laughing at Joanna's obvious conclusion. 'Don't be embarrassed, Joanna. I was a virgin, too, until I married Hugh.' She caught her husband's eye and grinned mischievously. 'Well . . . *almost*. Hugh *was* a bit of a stuffy bear in those day . . . I had to practically chain him to the bed to seduce him . . .'

Slightly shocked by her intimate revelation to an almost perfect stranger, Joanna looked at Julia's husband. He met her gaze squarely, the grey eyes filled with a mixture of wry resignation and serene amusement; the certainty of one who loves and is loved. 'You get used to it,' he said quietly, for her ears alone, revealing his perceptiveness. 'In fact, in time you begin to wonder how you lived without it.'

She knew immediately what he meant. Wasn't she even

now wondering how she would live without Richard? The question was, did she have the courage to live *with* him?

Before she could get to grips properly with the thought, Richard spoke. 'She's not really as embarrassed as she looks, are you, darling? Secretly, you adore all this attention. Under that prim, schoolmarm's skin is a closet exhibitionist who makes *me* look reticent!'

Joanna rose slowly to her feet, knowing she was responding to his deliberate provocation, but not caring. She was sick of his flippancy and jokes and manoeuvring and manipulating. He wanted her to take him seriously? She would take him seriously! She would give him *exhibitionist* . . .

She picked up her plate and held it high. Then she dumped the entire, still-steaming contents right into Richard's unprotected lap. He gave a yell, doubling over and dabbing frantically at the hot sauce with his napkin and, while he was doing that, she picked up the ice-water jug and poured the contents slowly, blissfully, all over his down-bent head. There wasn't a sound throughout the entire restaurant. Julia had a hand over her mouth. Hugh mopped up a splash of water from his sleeve. Only Ben ventured a comment . . . he laughed.

Exhilarated and appalled by the realisation of what he had driven her to, Joanna turned to run, but Richard was quicker. He vaulted to his feet, his hand flashing out, and suddenly Joanna was stranded in a blurry haze.

'Give them back, Richard,' she demanded furiously, conscious of the giggles and whispers now spreading out in waves across the room, especially from her pupils behind her.

Instead, her outstretched hand received a flesh and blood shackle. 'Hold the fort, will you, Hugh? I think this is Joanna's way of telling me she wants a private word . . .'

'I do *not*——' Joanna squirmed in his hold, only to be admonished.

'Don't overplay the scene, darling. You've already got

their attention——' He began to drag her between the
tables.

'I'm not going anywhere with you, Richard Marlow. Let
me go!' Her hopeless wail only prompted cheers and
catcalls from what she had mistakenly thought was a
sophisticated crowd of diners. 'My class . . . I can't leave my
class,' she said desperately.

'They haven't finished eating yet,' Richard pointed out
with aggravating truth as he propelled her out into the
watery winter sunlight, which diffused her remaining
vision even further. 'They'll be all right with Hugh and
Julia until we get back.'

'Back from where? I don't want to go anywhere!' She
stumbled a bare few steps in his wake before suddenly they
were in dimness again.

'Key, please . . .'

'Of course, Mr Marlow . . . er . . . shall you be requir-
ing . . .?'

'Not to be disturbed? Yes.' More steps. A whirr. A lurch.
She might not have perfect vision, but there was nothing
wrong with the rest of Joanna's senses.

'This is a *hotel*! Richard, is this a hotel? Where are we
going? I am *not* getting out of this lift!'

She tried to dig her heels in along the muffled hallway. 'If
you think I'm going into a room with you, you're very
much mistaken!'

As the door locked behind them she at last wrenched her
hand free. 'Richard, whatever stupid idea you've come up
with this time, it's not going to work. OK, so I was wrong
about Julia, I'm sorry, but that doesn't mean that it's right
for *us* . . .' She tried to summon up her previous conviction
but, somehow, the defiant gesture in the restaurant had
expended all her strength.

Thumps and bangs were her only answer. When she
stepped out cautiously to try and discover what he was
doing she found out. He was piling furniture around her.
'Richard, what are you *doing*?'

'Barricading you in,' he said in a slightly breathless voice.

'You're not walking out on me this time, not until we've talked, or rather, *you've listened* ...'

Oh, God! Despair whipped the foundations from under her temper. She knew all too well how vulnerable she was to Richard. Her pride and principles were precariously shaky. It was ironic that a love so strong could make her feel so wretchedly weak. Damn Richard! If he had been so intent on playing the lover, why hadn't he had the decency to put a bit of hollow-eyed realism into the character? Then at least she could have had the consolation of pretending to *herself* that she believed him. But no one in their right minds would believe that this confident, high-spirited, cheerful man bursting with rude health was pining for anyone's love!

'I should have thrown that plate in your face!' she said bitterly.

'Too hackneyed, darling. Your way had so much more originality and class—two of the things I love you for.'

Class? Who was he kidding? 'What are you doing?' she said suspiciously, hearing a faint rustling sound and trying to keep her mind strictly on practicalities.

'Taking ... off ... my ... jeans—ah, that's better. I'll just rinse them off and put them on the wall heater to dry out.'

'Dry out?' Joanna echoed hollowly. 'How long do you expect us to be here, for goodness sake?'

'I had to book the room overnight. They wouldn't let me take it for just a couple of hours, especially when I said we wouldn't have any luggage.'

'You tried to book this room for only a few hours?' Joanna shrieked. 'And of course they knew who you were! Oh, my God, what will people think?'

'I don't care what people think. People don't matter. Only we matter, you and I. If we have to stay all night, we will, but we're not leaving until you accept the truth.'

'That you're a low-down, lying snake?' Joanna spat at his shadowy outline.

'That I love you. And you love me.'

'It'll be a cold day in hell!'

'It is cold. It's winter. And every day without you is hell.'

The simplicity of the statement, as much as its inherent drama, got to her. 'Where are my glasses? I want my glasses back.' She couldn't bear to be at the mercy of that beautiful voice.

'You don't need them, Joanna. They won't help you see the truth. The truth is something you feel, not something you see.'

'Why are you doing this? What sort of satisfaction do you get from putting me though all this?' she whispered thickly. 'You're turning my whole life into some crazy farce and you think its funny.' A great wave of weariness swept over her and she closed her eyes against the pressure of the tears. 'It's not funny to me. I hate it. I just want to be left in peace!' It was a horrible lie, she knew it as she said it. Peace was boring, contentment was suffocation. Richard gave her life a certain flavour that it would never have again. He lit up her life and coloured it with his warmth. But, as essential as light and warmth were to life, one needed more . . . The tears flowed in earnest now and she didn't care. Let him see what he had done to her.

'Joanna? Darling? You're crying, you mustn't cry!' Richard sounded horrified, and she was glad and cried harder. Suddenly, the world came into hard, if watery, focus—her glasses thrust roughly on to her nose. Richard's face swam into her vision. He was as pale as his shirt. 'Don't cry, I didn't mean to hurt you. I'm so sorry, I must have been crazy. Here——' Bracing his good knee against the couch that ran along the front of her prison he reached over and lifted her with little apparent effort over the back of the couch and sat her on the soft pastel cushions, one hand taking hers, the other clumsily wiping at her tears with jerky motions. Richard—lovely, graceful, Richard— *awkward*?

Joanna blinked wet lashes and looked at him. He should have looked ridiculous, kneeling before her, barefooted, clad only in the loose white shirt with its drenched shoulders, but he didn't. For once, there wasn't a trace of humour about him. He looked his age ... a man approaching the peak of his maturity, a man who had sufficient experience of life to know what he valued and what would satisfy him. A man who had learned to trust his instincts. Joanna's eyes dried at the revolutionary thought. Had she been projecting her own fears on to his character? Did she *really* believe that a man with his sharp, insightful intelligence and mature artistic judgement could be emotionally immature? No ...

'Thank God you've stopped crying,' Richard said shakily, sitting back on his heels and reluctantly letting her hand drop. 'I feel like a prize bastard. It wasn't supposed to be like this ... look at me.' He lifted one hand, palm down. 'I'm trembling. The most important speech of my life and I've got stage fright. I feel hot and cold at the same time ... I'm sweating like a pig, and yet my skin feels like ice ...'

'Perhaps you didn't shake all the ice cubes out,' Joanna said faintly, shocked by the sight of Richard floundering for words.

'Don't joke,' he flared at her fiercely. 'For pity's sake, don't make a joke of me, Joanna!'

'Richard——' She wanted to tell him that it was all right.

'Oh, I know,' he cut in quickly, with a harsh laugh. 'That's rich, coming from me, right? Richard the clown!' He ran his hand through his damp hair. The gesture lifted the curved tails of his shirt over the taut, muscled thighs and Joanna jerked her eyes back to his face. This was no time to be confused by erotic longings, it could be the most important moment of her life.

'But, don't you see, darling?' he pleaded. 'I've only acted the way I have because its not in my nature to hide my feelings, and you make me feel ... on top of the world! From almost the first time we met, the rightness of our loving each other seemed so glaringly self-evident, that I thought that you couldn't help but realise it, too. I thought it was just a matter of time ... only I got impatient and tried to rush you.

'I know you think this has all happened too fast to trust,' he said, forcing himself to speak quietly. 'But, my darling, it's taken me twenty-eight years to find you, to find a woman who unmistakably prefers the private Richard to the public one, but who's strong enough to live with both of me. Joanna, until you came into my life I didn't even know what it was missing. Not just love ... but *you*, Joanna Carson. You complete me. We're two very different people and yet we *mesh*, like Hugh and Julia. Their marriage has its turbulent moments, it's bound too, but it's *enduring*, and intensely loving, and they're creating beautiful children from that love. That's what I want to do with you.'

He shifted on his heels and a flicker of genuine pain crossed his face. With a grimace of resignation he got stiffly to his feet then sat down beside her, massaging his scarred knee and flexing it experimentally. He hardly used his stick at all now, except, as Joanna would say, for effect, and sometimes the strain told.

'Damned thing. It's not because of this, is it? My being crippled?'

'Don't be ridiculous!' Her brown eyes snapped with outrage, and he smiled wryly at the removal of yet another possible obstacle. 'It's just that ... oh, Richard,' she said helplessly, '... you're so ... so ... *flamboyant* ...'

'You're afraid of being overwhelmed,' he finished for her, seeing her fears more clearly than she did, and understanding them. 'Have I ever done that?' She blushed, and he shrugged wryly. 'Aside from sex, I mean? Think about it. Every time I've tried to coerce or bully you what's happened? You've pushed back just as hard. Remember when I tried to make you take that part ... you overwhelmed *me*. But I trust you only to do that only in matters that are important to you, not just to score points. You'll always have my trust, Joanna, and I'll never betray yours. I'll always be open and honest with you, and I come from a long line of faithful husbands.'

Incredibly, in view of her past suspicions, she believed him, but Richard thought her silence a sceptical one.

'It's true. I confess that one of the reasons I brought you up here was to seduce you into giving me the answer I want, but I can't go through with it. I won't let myself have you, Joanna, if I can't have you *safe*. I'm not talking about vows or legalities, but about your happiness. It must be what you want, too. I know I tried to use sex before, to influence you, but that was because it was one way I was confident of reaching you. Sex is something that I know I'm good at——' He stopped abruptly as he realised how incredibly, swaggeringly arrogant that must sound and, to Joanna's secret and loving amusement, he went bright red.

'I get your point, Richard,' she said gently, letting him off the hook.

'Good.' The flush faded as he hurried into less dangerous waters. 'I was very much aware, you see, that there are things that a conventional nine-to-five man can offer you that I can't—anonymity, for one, although I can buy us privacy whenever we really need it, and a serene home life and the comfortable sterility—sorry, *stability*,' he corrected his deliberate error, 'of knowing that each day is going to be pretty much like the last. But, darling, you're not *made* for that kind of life. You wouldn't be happy, not really. You're made for challenge and bustle and excitement, and I can give you all of those. And I *can* offer you financial stability . . . I haven't invested all my money in this film, there's still an awful lot left . . . Hugh can confirm that——'

'Are you trying to *buy* my love?' Joanna was wide-eyed at the novel thought. Richard had actually doubted that *he* was worthy of *her*! He had doubted his ability to make her happy. How could he be so stupid? . . . so *blind*?

'Buy, beg, borrow, steal . . . anything. There'll have to be compromises, sure, but not sacrifices. I intend to make more films in New Zealand so you don't have to worry about career clashes . . . although later we might have to reorder our priorities, when the children are born. And if I do have to travel, well, we can worry about that later, but I promise you and the children will always come first.'

'Or at least a very close second,' said Joanna drily, not

wanting him to get entirely carried away. No, living with Richard would never be peaceful. It would be a rough ride, but a joyous one.

There was a fractional silence. 'Does that mean "yes"? You'll marry me?' His heart was in his jewel-bright eyes.

'No.' She felt a pang of guilt as his face bleached bone-white, and she quickly reached out to flick open his shirt buttons. 'It means I want you to make love to me. I like to try before I buy.' With a demure smile, she put her mouth against his naked chest, and felt the erratic vibration of his shock.

'Joanna!' He pulled her head violently back so that he could study her expression. She laughed huskily as she watched the paleness become tinged with colour, and the taut agony around his eyes and mouth melt and reform into hungry sensuality. The green eyes glowed with love and laughter. 'Bitch!' he whispered and tightened his hand in her hair. 'You *love* me.'

'I love you.' To say it aloud filled her with joy. It made all Richard's outrageousness of the past few weeks comprehensible. It made her feel outrageous, too. 'And yes, I'll marry you ... providing you can make me happy in bed.'

'Bed, hell, let's settle this thing here and now.' He pushed her down into the cushions and kissed her savagely, then more gently. '*Caveat emptor ...*' he murmured into her mouth.

'And what does this buyer have to beware of?' Joanna asked, stunned and excited at the speed and dexterity with which he was peeling off her clothes.

'Me. I drive a hard bargain,' he chuckled warmly, shifting his body to give her the proof. 'Oh God, that feels good ...' as hot skin met skin.

'We shouldn't really be doing this, not in the middle of a school trip,' Joanna gasped with a brief salute to common sense.

'We already are ...' His hands lifted and turned her naked body into his, a rust-coloured thigh moving heavily between hers and wedging firmly against the aching heart of her desire. His silk shirt pooled on the floor, followed by the nylon briefs that had barely contained his arousal. As his swollen manhood spilled out across her soft thighs, teasing her with his hot, velvety hardness, Joanna shivered.

'I'm going to teach you to fly with me, little virgin owl,' Richard promised in a purring growl, as he cupped her small breasts in his hands and nuzzled the soft crests into tight crests that melted in his mouth. 'Don't be afraid of falling, I'll be here to catch you. Soar with me, little one, wing-tip to wing-tip . . . let yourself go . . .'

His tongue sought her pulse-points, from temple to throat to breast to the soft silver nest that held her sweetest essence. He was not a silent lover, and his erotic urgings encouraged her to be vocal in response. He made each new and greater intimacy seem as lovingly natural as the last, so that the only shocks she felt were those of passionate delight. She flowed like honey in his arms and, by the time that he turned her on her back and slid a gentle hand between her legs to part her for his possession, he was shuddering with the effort to control his need, to take it slow for her sake.

'No, don't . . . I want you to see this,' he rasped, as she clumsily tried to brush off the spectacles she suddenly realised she was still wearing. 'I want you to see the way our differences complement each other . . .' And she did, as he lifted her hips to him, sweat breaking out across his strained face as he slowly eased himself into the sweet, tight sheath of her body. The pain was sharp but fleeting, and Joanna was soon frustrated by his restraint. She moved frantically, seeking relief from the building tension and Richard stiffened, arching his head back and groaning, the cords in his throat standing out rigidly. His eyes closed, then opened and sought hers. What he saw in their brown depths had him groaning out exultant words of pleasure as he exploded into a driving rhythm that became more powerful with each plunging stroke. Joanna could only follow where he lead her, sensing the imminent climax in the inner contractions of her own body, and in the muscles that shivered along Richard's spine and rippled across his perpiration-slicked chest and belly, culminating in one final, clenching thrust of his buttocks that propelled their joined bodies into a separate reality, a gloriously sweet delirium of the senses from which Joanna never wanted to recover.

Richard made her, though, by barely waiting until the after-tremors had dwindled to sweep her laughingly up in his arms and limp into the bedroom where he tossed her on to the extravagant softness of the bed. It rocked alarmingly.

'What did you expect, in the Honeymoon Suite?' grinned Richard wickedly as he joined her.

'*Richard!*' It was hard to look shocked when she felt so wonderful, and he was looking at her with those sexy, green, I'm-not-sated-yet eyes. Her body tingled its reawakening response.

'Hope, not arrogance,' he said, bending his head to lazily kiss one rosy nipple. Then he disappointed her by rolling over to pick up the telephone.

'Who are you ringing—the Press?' teased Joanna, running a finger over his hip-bone, revelling in her freedom to touch him.

'The Press later; my mother first.'

'Your *mother!*' She snatched her hand back, and he laughed and slid an arm around her narrow waist and scooped her back against him.

'Don't worry, she can't see us. But she's probably sitting beside her phone with bated breath. This was her idea, you know. I went crying to Mama when you turned me down and she came up trumps.'

'This was your *mother's* idea?' Joanna was scandalised. What kind of family was she marrying into?

'With a little input from me,' Richard murmured modestly, exploring the satiny smoothness of her shoulder, tucked against his chest. 'I told her all—well, almost all— including the fact that I knew you weren't indifferent to me. She said, what did I have to lose? She wants me to be happy, you see . . . and if I don't put her out of her misery now she'll probably ring later and interrupt some serious bargaining.' He chuckled lecherously. 'She did that to us once before, remember . . . if she hadn't I might have swept you off your feet weeks ago!'

And missed all this excitement? Never! Joanna thought with delicious amusement. She lay curled against his side, listening to Richard's short but happy conversation with his mother. She had the feeling that once she got over her embarrassment she was going to like Constance Marlow. No, she was going to *love* Constance Marlow. She was going to love all the Marlows, existing and to come. She was a Marlow now herself, self-christened next door in the restaurant, with all the dramatic flair that befitted the name!

Harlequin Presents

Coming Next Month

Available in March wherever paperback books are sold, or through Harlequin Reader Service:

In the U.S.
901 Fuhrmann Blvd.
P.O. Box 1397
Buffalo, N.Y. 14240-1397

In Canada
P.O. Box 603
Fort Erie, Ontario
L2A 5X3

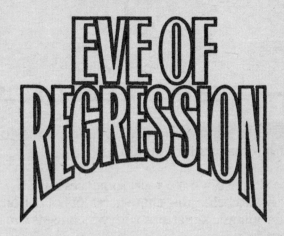

MAIL-IN-OFFER

OFFER CERTIFICATE ✂

I have enclosed the required number of proofs of purchase from any specially marked "Gifts From The Heart" Harlequin romance book, plus cash register receipts and a check or money order payable to Harlequin Gifts From The Heart Offer, to cover postage and handling.

002

CHECK ONE	ITEM	# OF PROOFS OF PURCHASE	POSTAGE & HANDLING FEE
	01 Brass Picture Frame	2	$ 1.00
	02 Heart-Shaped Candle Holders with Candles	3	$ 1.00
	03 Heart-Shaped Keepsake Box	4	$ 1.00
	04 Gold-Plated Heart Pendant	5	$ 1.00
	05 Collectors' Doll Limited quantities available	12	$ 2.75

NAME _____

STREET ADDRESS _____ APT. # _____

CITY _____ STATE _____ ZIP _____

Mail this certificate, designated number of proofs of purchase (inside back page) and check or money order for postage and handling to:

Gifts From The Heart, P.O. Box 4814
Reidsville, N. Carolina 27322-4814

NOTE THIS IMPORTANT OFFER'S TERMS

Requests must be postmarked by May 31, 1988. Only proofs of purchase from specially marked "Gifts From The Heart" Harlequin books will be accepted. This certificate plus cash register receipts and a check or money order to cover postage and handling must accompany your request and may not be reproduced in any manner. Offer void where prohibited, taxed or restricted by law. LIMIT ONE REQUEST PER NAME, FAMILY, GROUP, ORGANIZATION OR ADDRESS. Please allow up to 8 weeks after receipt of order for shipment. Offer only good in the U.S.A. Hurry—Limited quantities of collectors' doll available. Collectors' dolls will be mailed to first 15,000 qualifying submitters. All other submitters will receive 12 free previously unpublished Harlequin books and a postage & handling refund.

OFFER-1RR

ATTRACTIVE, SPACE SAVING BOOK RACK

Display your most prized novels on this handsome and sturdy book rack. The hand-rubbed walnut finish will blend into your library decor with quiet elegance, providing a practical organizer for your favorite hard-or soft-covered books.

Only $9.95

Approximately 16" x 8" when assembled

Assembles in seconds!

To order, rush your name, address and zip code, along with a check or money order for $10.70* ($9.95 plus 75¢ postage and handling) payable to *Harlequin Reader Service*:

Harlequin Reader Service
Book Rack Offer
901 Fuhrmann Blvd.
P.O. Box 1396
Buffalo, NY 14269-1396

Offer not available in Canada.

BKR-1A

*New York and Iowa residents add appropriate sales tax.

GIFTS FROM THE HEART

from Harlequin

FREE BY MAIL With proofs of purchase plus postage and handling

A. Hand-polished solid brass picture frame 1-5/8″ × 1-3/8″ with 2 proofs of purchase.

B. Individually handworked, pair of heart-shaped glass candle holders (2″ diameter), 6″ candles included, with 3 proofs of purchase.

C. Heart-shaped porcelain keepsake box (1″ high) with delicate flower motif with 4 proofs of purchase.

D. Radiant gold-plated heart pendant on 16″ chain with complimentary satin pouch with 5 proofs of purchase.

E. Beautiful collectors' doll with genuine porcelain face, hands and feet, and a charming heart appliqué on dress with 12 proofs of purchase. Limited quantities available. See offer terms.

HERE IS HOW TO GET YOUR FREE GIFTS

Send us the required number of proofs of purchase (below) of specially marked ''Gifts From The Heart'' Harlequin books and cash register receipts with the Offer Certificate (available in the back pages) properly completed, plus a check or money order (do not send cash) payable to Harlequin Gifts From The Heart Offer. We'll RUSH you your specified gift. Hurry—Limited quantities of collectors' doll available. See offer terms.

101R

GIFTS FROM THE HEART
ONE PROOF OF PURCHASE

To collect your free gift by mail you must include the necessary number of proofs of purchase with order certificate.